Earline

8-25-05 C.A.

BW

"I don't have time for questions today," Greg said sternly. "I've got things to do."

Jane was certain she'd never met a harder-headed, more stubborn man in her life. He might not want a wife now, or ever. Well, she wasn't so darn sure she wanted him for a husband either. So why was she continuing to plead her case?

"Sounds like copping out to me," she complained, her temper simmering, threatening to erupt. "Of course, what you really mean is that you won't *take* time. Odd, since you *are* the one who advertised for a wife—remember?"

Greg's shoulders shifted in an exaggerated droop. "Who's going to let me forget?"

D0967464

Kate Denton is a pseudonym for the Texas writing team of Carolyn Hake and Jeanie Lambright. Friends as well as co-authors, they concur for the most part on politics and good Mexican restaurants, but disagree about men—tall versus short—and what constitutes good weather—sun versus showers. One thing they do agree on, though, is the belief that romance is not just for the young!

Don't miss any of our special offers. Write to us at the following address for information on our newest releases.

Harlequin Reader Service
U.S.: 3010 Walden Ave., P.O. Box 1325, Buffalo, NY 14269
Canadian: P.O. Box 609, Fort Erie, Ont. L2A 5X3

Mail-Order Mother
Kate Denton

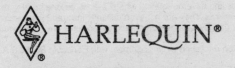

HARLEQUIN®

TORONTO · NEW YORK · LONDON
AMSTERDAM · PARIS · SYDNEY · HAMBURG
STOCKHOLM · ATHENS · TOKYO · MILAN · MADRID
PRAGUE · WARSAW · BUDAPEST · AUCKLAND

Read 5/14/2011 Good

If you purchased this book without a cover you should be aware that this book is stolen property. It was reported as "unsold and destroyed" to the publisher, and neither the author nor the publisher has received any payment for this "stripped book."

TO MILDRED SUTTON
A VERY SPECIAL LADY

ISBN 0-373-03510-1

MAIL-ORDER MOTHER

First North American Publication 1998.

Copyright © 1998 by Kate Denton.

All rights reserved. Except for use in any review, the reproduction or utilization of this work in whole or in part in any form by any electronic, mechanical or other means, now known or hereafter invented, including xerography, photocopying and recording, or in any information storage or retrieval system, is forbidden without the written permission of the publisher, Harlequin Enterprises Limited, 225 Duncan Mill Road, Don Mills, Ontario, Canada M3B 3K9.

All characters in this book have no existence outside the imagination of the author and have no relation whatsoever to anyone bearing the same name or names. They are not even distantly inspired by any individual known or unknown to the author, and all incidents are pure invention.

This edition published by arrangement with Harlequin Books S.A.

® and TM are trademarks of the publisher. Trademarks indicated with ® are registered in the United States Patent and Trademark Office, the Canadian Trade Marks Office and in other countries.

Printed in U.S.A.

CHAPTER ONE

"Rancher seeks wife, mother
for infant twins. Contact
Box 826, Martinsville, Texas..."

"Now doesn't that beat all? This guy must be a real winner." Cerise Henley's mock-serious recitation of the advertisement in the *Amarillo Times* and her cynical analysis brought snickers from four of her colleagues clustered together in canvas director chairs.

Jane Jarrett, however, found nothing amusing in the situation. She eyed the group with rising indignation.

"Any takers?" Cerise asked derisively, folding the paper and tossing it to Angela.

"Sounds *terribly* appealing," Angela gibed, perusing the item, which Cerise had circled with a ballpoint pen.

"Reminds me of something from the nineteenth century," Bonnie chimed in. "When women were scarce and had to be ordered in like farm equipment or sacks of flour."

"At least he's taking control of his life," Jane huffed, snatching the newspaper when it came her way. "Rather brave I'd say."

Ignoring the questioning stares of the others, Jane stuffed the paper into her tote bag. Admirable, too,

5

she thought with envy, sensitive to the fact that at the moment, she didn't feel one bit in control of her own life, which seemed to be falling apart before her very eyes.

The latest blow had come only yesterday with the news that Carvel Inc. was dumping "J.J."—as Jane was known professionally—as its featured spokesperson. This photo shoot near the rugged Palo Duro Canyon in the Texas Panhandle would be her last modeling assignment campaign for the cosmetics giant.

Carvel's rationale for not renewing her contract was that they were seeking a younger image. Would Cerise or Angela or one of these other twenty-somethings be her replacement? *Well, be my guest,* she wanted to say, because—aside from the jolt of being considered "over the hill" at age thirty-three—Jane couldn't care less who replaced her.

Work no longer satisfied. Jane had begun noticing the signs of classic burnout even before the Carvel notice. She wasn't sure what direction her life should take, but there would be no teary regrets if modeling was excluded from it.

The day drew on at a snail's pace. Jane waited for the photographer to set up, posed as instructed, smiled on cue and watched while the other models did the same. She was cautious not to reveal a hint of boredom or bitterness, or to be anything but the consummate professional. This might be her last gig with Carvel, but she was going out with the same kind of fervid dedication that had been a major reason for her rise to the top.

Only later that evening, ensconced in her hotel

suite, solitude secured, did she allow herself to dwell once more on her future...and the past.

Slumping back onto the bed, she pulled her knees to her chest. *How did I become a walking target for fate's little zingers?* First, the breakup of her marriage, now the derailment of her career. Tough to handle, but she could have borne those distressing defeats if it weren't for...for...

Tears began to well in her eyes. She still couldn't come to terms with that other blow—the knowledge that she was unable to bear children. Barren. Such an ugly word.

Months had elapsed, but the shattering prognosis rang in her ears as though it were yesterday. After being married for five years and trying to conceive for three, she'd seen a specialist. "I'm ninety-nine percent sure you'll never become pregnant," the gynecologist said. "All the treatments or surgeries in the world won't make a difference."

Kevin, her husband, found her infertility too big a deficiency to overlook and used it as one of his excuses for walking out. He hadn't even stuck around long enough to question the doctor's opinion, or wait for a second one. Not that it mattered. Jane had both questioned and sought other views; all were the same.

So...no baby, no marriage and now no career. Jane leaned dejectedly against the headboard of the bed and wondered what she, like the rancher, could do to take control, get her life on track again. Her eyes moved to the newspaper section that she'd absentmindedly pitched onto the nightstand—the sec-

tion with the rancher's ad. She picked it up, quickly
put it down, then picked it up again and studied it.

Okay, the ad was unusual, intriguing actually, in
what it left unsaid. But who in her right mind would
give it more than a passing thought? *Me? No way.*

Jane sat for an hour going over the ramifications.
The longer she tried to emphasize the absurdity of
what she was contemplating, the stronger the possibilities became. The rancher's life was in turmoil...so was hers. He was obviously having difficulty finding a woman...she'd recently lost her
man. The rancher needed a mother for his children...and she needed to be a mother. The situation
seemed heaven-sent. Karma. Kismet. Destiny.

"Hesitate and you are lost," she reminded herself, knowing if she waited much longer, what
would be lost would be her nerve. Before that could
happen, she grabbed some personal stationery from
her briefcase, penned a quick response and rang for
a bellman to post the letter.

It was dark when Greg Merrifield drove along the
farm road toward home. His van lights illuminated
the scrolled iron arches leading to his ranch as he
negotiated the turn. Time had gotten away from him
at the livestock auction; now he chided himself for
missing the babies' dinner. Sure they were being
well cared for by Helga, the housekeeper. And
Elton, his foreman, and Elton's wife, Nita, were always nearby in case of an emergency. But that
wasn't good enough. The twins needed a parent
there.

They were asleep in their beds when he sent

Helga on her way and went up to kiss them good-night. Neither woke as he brushed their velvety faces with his lips, but Sarah's rosebud mouth puckered and Sean's tiny snores momentarily quietened. Greg came downstairs, microwaved the meat loaf dinner left for him and carried his plate to the table. As he ate, he thought back to his children.

Nearing fifteen months, Sean and Sarah were the light of his life. If it hadn't been for them... He shook his head. The babies had gotten him through those awful days following Charlotte's death, had made him realize that life does go on, as he witnessed a first tooth, a first step, a first "Da Da." Those two, just by their mere presence, had brought joy back into his existence.

Part of him was convinced they could be happy forever, just the three of them. But part of him...a part he tried to tune out...acknowledged that the children needed more. Specifically they needed a mother. That's why he'd placed that stupid advertisement. That, along with everyone nagging him, telling him the time had come to remarry, to give Sean and Sarah that mother. Even Charlotte's voice nagged him—and she'd been gone over a year now.

It was Charlotte's dying wish that he remarry, provide her children a mother. If she'd only foreseen how burdensome that wish would turn out, Greg was certain she'd never have insisted he honor it. But she had—and he'd agreed—and now he felt obligated.

He picked up the packet of letters he'd retrieved from his post office box that afternoon and had tossed onto the table. Answers to the ad. At a minimum, there were twenty, about eighteen more than he'd anticipated. Plucking an envelope from the pile, he ripped it open.

A few days later Greg had winnowed his way down to the last one. The ad had produced precisely what he'd expected—nothing. Not one of the women he'd contacted had piqued his interest. Just as none of the local women had stirred him. Plenty had tried...and tried again, some of them acting as if they hungered desperately for a man. Occasionally Greg felt like a crippled calf being scrutinized by a flock of impatient vultures.

That wasn't what he was looking for. He wanted a...a partner, a parenting partner. Not some idealistic female oozing with romantic notions, but a sensible woman who shared his commitment to being a parent. That's why he'd reluctantly gone along when Elton had promoted the ad. But it wasn't working. Thank goodness this experiment would soon be over and he could get back to his life and his children. As soon as he dealt with this last letter.

Two more rings and the answering machine will start up. Greg ought to know. He'd been through this routine four times already. One ring left. *Ah, sweet relief.* He'd promised Elton five tries and five it was. He hadn't promised to leave messages and wait for the woman to call back. Greg picked up a pen. The final name to cross off his—

"Hello."

Damnation. The voice was live, not a recording. Greg uttered a silent curse. Almost off the hook with Elton's harebrained scheme, now he was caught.

"Hello?" she repeated.

"Oh, uh, Jane Jarrett, please."

"Speaking."

"This is Greg Merrifield," he said. "You answered my ad."

Jane groaned and momentarily considered hanging up. All week she'd been wishing she could retrieve her hastily mailed letter. It'd been an impulsive act—temporary insanity, pure and simple. Her troubles couldn't be fixed by marrying a perfect stranger, that's for sure. Women didn't get husbands, create instant families, via newspaper advertisements. The thought of a family gave her pause. The ad had said twins. Not just one but *two* babies... Jane so wanted a baby.

She dropped onto the couch, phone in hand.

"Are you still there, Miss Jarrett?"

"...Yes. I didn't expect to hear from you so soon," she said, her voice polite, but strained. "I only mailed the letter Tuesday."

"I received it Wednesday and today's Friday. Now that the calendar's taken care of, can we move on? Your address says Dallas. How did you happen upon an ad in an Amarillo newspaper?" he asked.

"I was there on business...spotted it in the classifieds."

"Travelers don't usually read the classifieds."

"Oh, it just caught my eye," Jane said evasively. She wasn't about to reveal the scenario that had preceded its arrival into her hands.

"And what prompted you to answer?" This

woman sounded cultured, sophisticated, with barely a trace of a Texas accent. What could compel her to consider taking on a family in Martinsville of all places?

"I answered because I'm ready to be a mother."

And what's wrong with the customary method? he wondered. If Jane looked half as good as she sounded, suitors shouldn't be a problem.

"How old are your twins?" she asked.

"Almost fifteen months."

"Boys or girls?"

"One of each."

"How wonderful."

Greg stiffened. He didn't want her going gaga over the babies. Women tended to do that, to think of children as cute little dolls, and motherhood as a state of sublime bliss where reality dared not enter. Likely this woman was no different. "Responding to an ad like mine is rather daring," he said, realizing he was letting his end of the conversation lag.

"No more so than placing one."

"It seemed the most expedient thing to do. You see I live on a large ranch out in the middle of nowhere." *There, that's a good approach. Nice, but not one whit encouraging.*

"'The middle of nowhere'? Now that's intriguing," she said. Her caller was courteous, his whispery voice tantalizing, but Jane was getting vibes that said the man didn't give a rat's tail about sparking her interest.

"Not intriguing to most people," he scoffed, reinforcing her impressions. "The Panhandle is an acquired taste, Miss Jarrett. It doesn't have a lot of pizzazz and definitely no glamour."

To Greg's surprise she chuckled. "No glamour? I think I can cope with that." *I've had enough glamour to last a lifetime.*

"Are you always this agreeable?"

"Not always. Would you prefer disagreeable?"

Now he chuckled. "No, agreeable is okay."

She liked that laugh. Rumbling...as if it came from down deep.

There was an extended silence, with neither speaking. "Uh," Jane began, "your wife...may I—?"

Her cadence was careful, making Greg feel that she understood the pain that came with talking about loss, pain that was easing for him, but hadn't altogether vanished. It still lurked in the recesses of his heart and Greg wondered whether it would ever go away completely. Still, he hadn't planned to go into detail about Charlotte. "She died last year." His words were drawn out, hesitant.

"I'm sorry."

"Yeah."

"So you've decided to remarry?"

"If the right woman comes along," Greg answered, regaining his equilibrium. He didn't need to make explanations to a stranger, dammit, especially one he hadn't anticipated on talking to at all. "Listen, Miss Jarrett, now that we've met—so to speak—I'll think this over and decide whether we'll suit. Maybe I'll get back to you. Thanks for your time." He hung up.

Dumbfounded, Jane stared at the phone, certain

she'd never hear from the man again. That last speech had sounded like a "Don't call us, we'll call you" brush-off. Her first reaction was one of anger, the second relief at having been saved from her own impulsiveness.

Padding into the kitchen in her stocking feet, she replayed the conversation in her head, all the while wondering why she bothered. She was rid of the guy. She should be grateful. *Yet he sounded...* "Sexy. That's how he sounded," Jane said aloud. "So what? I'm still not interested." *Not in the slightest.*

Two days went by with no further word. Jane knew it was unrealistic to expect a return call. *You don't want one—remember?* So why then did she dash to the phone every time it rang? And why did her brain keep rehashing their brief exchange? It defied logic. But Jane had to admit her curiosity was stoked. So much so she was bursting to share her tale.

Thus it was that during a yogurt break with her sister Melissa at a shopping mall, Jane revealed the recent chain of events—the ad, her letter, the phone call.

The manic expression on her sister's face told Jane she should have confided in someone else. Instead of some much-needed, cold-water-in-the-face admonition to get a grip, Melissa—always the dreamer—clasped her hands together enthusiastically. "How exciting! I can picture him now. Riding a huge palomino...skin bronzed by the Texas sun, a slight squint to his steely gaze—"

"Oh, sure. Mel, do you realize you're describing

Roy Rogers? Remember him in those old Western movies Daddy used to watch? More than likely this guy rides a broken-down pickup and has a complexion like a football. Not that it would matter of course,'' Jane added quickly.

''Uh-huh.'' Melissa's eyes narrowed suspiciously. ''So you're saying you're not a teeny bit curious?'' She measured off a quarter inch between her thumb and forefinger.

Melissa is too perceptive. ''It's an outlandish notion,'' Jane hedged.

''So? It might be just the medicine you need. At least you'd be *doing* something instead of moping around your apartment for days on end. Even if it is just to the mall, this is the first afternoon I've gotten you out in weeks.''

Fortunately Melissa spotted a half-price shoe sale and the subject was forgotten. Or so Jane thought. As they were parting later, Melissa squeezed her arm and said, ''I think you should check out your mysterious rancher. What have you got to lose?''

The possibilities nagged at Jane during the drive back to her condo. What *did* she have to lose? All her life a home, a family, had been Jane Jarrett's foremost goal. Not being famous, not making scads of money, not having her picture plastered on the covers of dozens of women's magazines. All that had been window dressing while she waited for her real dreams to unfold. Now those dreams were shattered, possibly beyond repair. An emptiness gnawed at her, an emptiness she had no way of filling. Unless...

Jane had to admit Melissa had a point. She

should check out Greg Merrifield, if for no other reason than to prove he wasn't someone who got his kicks trolling for unsuspecting women and enticing them to do who knows what. She'd have Stan, her attorney, look into his background. Ensure that the man was what he claimed to be. After all, he did have her address and telephone number— her private, unlisted number.

Stan performed a cursory investigation confirming the existence of Gregory Merrifield, owner of a ranch, the Circle G. A solid member of the Martinsville community. Not a predator at all—at least not a known one—and exactly who he said he was.

Jane had an inexplicable longing to put a face to the name and details, to learn more about the children. *"Quit being a nincompoop,"* she reprimanded, the influence of Melissa's contagious encouragement beginning to wear off.

Yet Jane couldn't stop dwelling on the mystical properties of such a relationship. All week long she'd lectured herself that having the advertisement literally dropped in her lap was sheer coincidence and that she was fortunate her response hadn't triggered something more troublesome than a phone call. The lectures failed to work. She simply couldn't dispel the possibility that some sort of divine intervention was bringing her, Greg Merrifield and the twins together.

So engrossed was she in the preordained-family concept that Jane refused two new modeling opportunities. Ron Gold, her agent, fussed and fumed and issued dire warnings about her making a "gigantic career blunder,'' but Jane held her ground. She would not be able to focus on a job until she got this fixation out of her system.

Looking to do precisely that, Jane agreed to a Cancún vacation with a group of girlfriends. A week in a touristy environment might be therapeutic, even fun. At the last minute, however, she canceled out, the prospect of so much nonstop togetherness unpalatable.

You must do something to end this obsession, Jane finally decided. It was Friday again, a whole week since she'd talked to Greg Merrifield and he was still on her mind. Maybe if she could speak to him once more. *Well, why not?* Getting his phone number shouldn't be a major hurdle. Martinsville was a small place and she doubted people there were big on unlisted numbers. She lifted the receiver and dialed Information. Sure enough, it took only an instant.

''Merrifield.''

''Jane Jarrett.'' She got right to the point. ''Have you decided yet whether 'we'll suit'?''

Greg smiled in spite of himself, then immediately caught himself. This wasn't some innocuous male-female repartee, the woman was serious. ''Actually, I've questioned if placing that ad was a lapse in judgment. Probably I should apologize for bothering you to begin with.''

Jane almost lashed out at him. Getting her attention, then leading her on like that...*whoa, slow down.* It was probably better he *was* having reservations; most reasonable people would.

More collected now, Jane said, ''A lapse in judgment's exactly what I accused myself of after I answered the ad. But the longer I thought about it, the more potential I saw in your plan. Surely you were sincere when you set out on this course.''

''I was trying to meet my obligations,'' he said. ''Have my children grow up with two parents.''

''That's admirable of you,'' she said, meaning it. The man had to have some good qualities if he was concerned enough about the twins having a mother to seek out a stranger. ''All I'm asking is for you to get to know me before rejecting me out of hand.''

He seemed to be mulling over her request. Anyway, that's what Jane assumed from the dead air at the other end of the line.

''Your letter didn't provide much information,'' he said eventually.

This coming from a man who'd placed a three-line ad. ''No,'' she said, ''but I'll be glad to answer all your questions, tell you anything you want to know. Just ask.'' Jane felt her heart racing.

Greg had to bite his tongue to keep from blurting out ''Tell me everything.'' Which was ridiculous. About as ridiculous as the way the woman had monopolized his thoughts all week. He'd reread her sparse note half a dozen times and picked up the phone more than once to call her again since their brief conversation.

Why had she spurred his interest when no one else had managed to? Not the veterinarian's assistant who was constantly sidling up to him, not the grocer's daughter who was knitting winter sweaters for the babies, not the schoolteacher who'd brought out enough pies and cakes to sustain a six-week sugar binge. And certainly not any of the other women who'd replied to his ad.

"Well?" Jane prompted.

"Okay, let's see..." Gad, he should have developed a script for this. "Have you ever been married?"

"Yes...married for five years...divorced seven months ago."

"Hmm," Greg responded.

"What does that hmm mean?" she asked.

"Only that I'm puzzled as to why you're eager to tie the knot again so soon. A lot of people would be gun-shy. This isn't a rebound thing, is it? A way to get even with your ex-husband?"

"No," she answered. At this point, Jane hadn't really delved into her underlying motivations. But she knew positively that they had nothing to do with Kevin. So why was she so determined about pursuing this? There were the children, of course. And...and... "Don't you have any more questions?"

Oh, yeah, Greg thought, a million of them. *Thankfully I've got better sense than to ask them.* As sure as God made little green apples, he knew that a couple of steps more and he'd be ankle-deep in quicksand. Even from a four-hundred-mile distance, the intoxicating effect Jane had on him made him light-headed. He might need a wife, but he had no intention of putting his heart in jeopardy. He should nip this conversation in the bud. "I guess I'm too tired to think of any more," he said. "It's late and I'm exhausted."

Jane looked at her clock radio. It was barely nine. "Is this your way of brushing me off?"

"No, of course not." He sounded unconvincing even to himself. "Remember you're talking to a rancher. We rise with the roosters and hit the sack before the owls are on the prowl. Besides, I've been pretty busy with this ad thing, too," he added, lavishly embellishing on the truth.

Busy indeed. Probably with a crush of other applicants. Inexplicably Jane had ruled out competition. The way her luck was running lately there was probably a line of women three blocks long all panting to be Mrs. Merrifield.

Just thinking about being beaten out sent Jane's hopes plummeting. She hadn't even gotten to first base. And Merrifield wasn't having "lapses" in judgment as he'd claimed; he was merely passing over her.

"This isn't fair." Jane felt herself dangerously close to whining. "I'm entitled to a decent hearing."

"Oh, says who?" His tone was now frosty and Jane knew she was coming on too strong.

"Please reconsider," she pleaded. "Just give me the courtesy of an interview…anytime you say. Being a mother is more important to me than anything else in the whole world."

He paused again. *You're a damn fool, Merrifield.* But the sincerity in her voice and the message that came with it were impossible to ignore. Brusquely, he said, "This isn't something that can be handled by telephone. If you're really as gung ho as you say you are, then you can have your interview. But you have to be willing to come out here.''

Her pulse quickened. ''When?''

''Wednesday. That's my first free minute. Since you're so keen on mothering, you ought to see what you might be signing up for.''

''True enough.''

They spoke for as long as it took Greg Merrifield to give directions to his ranch and Jane to write them down. Then he rang off.

She was opening a frozen dinner when he called again. ''One more thing…'' he started in, not giving his name. But then he didn't have to; Jane had already memorized his voice. ''Just to let you know—give you fair warning. This doesn't guarantee a commitment on my part.''

''Nor on mine.''

''Could be a wasted effort, a wild-goose chase.''

''I'll take that risk,'' she said. For the first time in months, a genuine smile spread across Jane's face.

CHAPTER TWO

JANE ripped off her print dress and flung it across the bed. *Too busy.* She eyed her red Chanel suit on the hanger. *Too dressy.* Pity she hadn't shopped for something new because nothing she owned seemed appropriate. She stared helplessly into the walk-in closet teeming with clothes. How did one dress to impress when the position was wife and mother and the "impressee" an unknown?

Finally, she settled on a royal blue suit. The hue complemented her eyes, also blue, and the bright color would appeal to the children. Who are you kidding, she asked herself. *You know this is a man-pleaser outfit—short skirt, curvy lines...*

Jane pushed the thought aside and glanced at her watch. She needed to move on. It was nearing six a.m. and she had a plane to catch. *Why did I agree to a seven o'clock flight?*

Arriving at the Amarillo airport later that morning, Jane obtained a rental car for the rest of her journey. As she headed toward her destination, her nerves shifted into overdrive. She checked the directions she'd scribbled on a notepad while talking with Greg Merrifield. The Martinsville exit should be appearing any second.

Jane tried for what must have been the hundredth time to picture the rancher. All she had to go on was his phone voice. Slightly raspy, slightly mocking, totally sexy—with the whispery quality of a young Clint Eastwood. Unlike women who swooned over bedroom eyes or gawked at taut gym-toned bodies, Jane was more readily captivated by a man's nonvisual attributes. Intelligence, a sense of humor...and the way he spoke. Yes, Jane definitely liked listening to Greg Merrifield talk.

She studied the directions again. *Something is not right.* She'd driven through Pampa thirty minutes ago and according to the instructions she should have come upon the turnoff before now. Accepting the inevitable, Jane stopped at a gas station for assistance and discovered she'd driven at least twenty miles past her exit.

Retracing her path, she finally sighted the road to Martinsville with its marker sign lying on the ground, passed through the small, unassuming town and sped toward the Circle G. Gripping the steering wheel, her palms began to sweat and she increased the air conditioner flow. She was late.

''Well, that's that,'' Greg said to Elton, gesturing toward the antique clock on the fireplace mantel. ''Jane Jarrett should have been here an hour ago. Apparently she's not coming after all. She probably looked Martinsville up on the map and decided we're too far out in the boonies for her to bother.''

Greg placed his baby daughter in the playpen beside her twin brother. ''I've got work to do,'' he announced, trying to appear unperturbed when in truth he felt befuddled—a combination of getting off the hook, yet being let down. ''I've wasted too much energy on that woman as it is.''

"And if she *does* show?" Elton asked.

"Then get rid of her. Tell her we've found someone else. Someone who understands punctuality."

"But *we* haven't," the agitated foreman reminded.

"So? She won't know that. It'll be our little secret. Admit it, Elton, advertising was a rotten idea. The smart thing is to forget the ad and concede defeat."

The more Greg had anticipated the meeting with Jane, the more his misgivings had grown. Eventually he'd find a wife. But on his own terms, his own schedule.

"Then what?"

Greg looked at his foreman questioningly.

"Don't pretend with me, Greg. You know what I'm getting at. You've rebuffed every woman who's even batted her eyes at you. And you haven't given chase to anyone, either. I never thought I'd see the day when Greg Merrifield would go back on his word."

"Don't you think that's hitting below the belt?"

"What do you call it then? Over a year now and no wife in sight. When Charlotte asked you to make sure her babies grew up with a mother, she wasn't talking about a live-in nanny. You swore you'd see to it."

Greg sucked in a breath. "I didn't realize there was a statute of limitations on a promise. Surely a little longer isn't going to make a difference. This just isn't something I can deal with yet. I need more time."

"Friend, you're running out of time. Those kids

of yours will be in college before you make a move.''

"I know, I know. I'll think of something."

"Talk's cheap."

"Well maybe my fairy godmother will step in and find me someone!"

"This Jarrett woman could be that someone if you'd give her half a chance. Doesn't seem right...you rejecting her sight unseen."

"She's not here. Remember?"

"So what if she shows up?" Elton's brow furrowed in distress as he restated his original question.

"Then *you* talk to her. If you approve, I'll meet her myself when I get back. Right now I need to run into town for diapers. We're down to the last package—"

"Hold on!" Elton barked. "What do you mean, if *I* approve?"

"Look her over. Feel her out. You can handle this as well as I can, probably better."

"Gosh darn it," his foreman grumbled. "My job's handling your cattle, not prospective wives."

"Well you did a good job picking out Nita, so you oughta be up to this, too. Just consider it another pesky chore, like mucking out the barn or dealing with that contrary bull we bought from the Reisners. Speaking of the Reisners, I need to head up there for a spell before I go to town. Ken wants to sell some more of his herd."

"Gosh darn it," Elton repeated lamely. He put a hand on Greg's shoulder and stared him in the eye. "You've known Jane Jarrett was coming all week.

You don't have to run a bunch of piddling errands *now*.''

"Like I said, Miss Jarrett isn't here. And no way do I plan to sit around waiting for her to arrive at her convenience.''

Elton tightened his grip. "If she comes and I do this, can I count on you to cooperate?''

Resignation ragged Greg's voice. "Do I have a choice with you *and* her breathing down my neck?''

"Not as I see it.''

The sight of the welcoming Circle G archway and the bucolic pastures framing the private road did nothing to allay Jane's rising panic. *You can't afford to weaken,* she told herself. No matter what, once she started something, she saw it through. Even exploring uncharted territory—like now—she couldn't abandon the quest. This might be her only crack at motherhood, at forming a family of her own.

Pep talk aside, by the time she stopped the car in front of the sprawling two-story house with its wooden rail fence and well-groomed lawn, the risks in the venture, along with her dread of coming face-to-face with Greg Merrifield, had Jane trembling. She wasn't comforted by the reaction of the man ambling out of the front door and—hands stuffed into jeans pockets—giving her the once-over.

A shocked disappointment crossed his face and he made no attempt to disguise it as she approached the front porch.

Jane stopped in her tracks and contemplated a

hasty retreat to the car. The man was sizing her up and reacting as though she didn't come anywhere near meeting his standards. Talk about gall. He was no prize himself; in fact, the grizzled cowboy was the polar opposite of his sexy phone voice—and old enough to be her father.

"Well come on up," he coaxed, gesturing her to the shade of the porch. "Sorry. Forgot my manners, I guess...staring like that. But you're so..." He hastily thrust out a hand. "I'm Elton Jones, Circle G foreman."

Jane breathed a quick sigh of relief at her mistake and accepted the handshake. "Jane Jarrett. I'm happy to meet you, but where's Mr. Merrifield?"

The foreman cleared his throat, then ran a palm across his balding pate. "When an hour passed and you hadn't showed, he got it in his head you'd stood him up and took off to handle a couple of things. Just as well, too. Let's get in out of this heat and I'll explain."

Jane, confused and mightily exasperated, followed the foreman through an open door and down a long entryway. The house was old, possibly fifty, seventy-five years, but updated with whitewashed paneling, modern ceiling fans and recessed lighting.

He led her into a large family room where two babies played in an oversize playpen. "They're about ready for a nap."

"Oh, how adorable," she cried uninhibitedly, delighted at the faces turned her way. "May I hold one of them?"

"Well, uh, sure. But they're teething—back molars I think, so watch out for drool." He eyed her suit warily. "I'd hate to see your pretty clothes all messed up."

"Not a problem. What's a little drool between friends?"

She lifted a baby as Elton motioned her to a chair. "That's Sean," he said.

"I have something in my bag I think he'll like," she said, smiling indulgently as Sean pulled at her shiny suit button. She withdrew a stuffed green frog and Sean abandoned her button to latch onto it.

"And I have a turtle for his sister," Jane said, gazing over at the other baby.

"Sarah," Elton said.

Dressed in a pale pink pinafore and beginning to doze off in the playpen, the chubby girl resembled a sleeping cherub. A surge of emotion sprang into Jane's soul. *Could anything be more precious than these two?*

"Appears as if you've had experience with children," Elton said, smiling at the turtle Jane handed to him.

Jane nodded. "Brothers and sisters, plus several close nieces and nephews. Big family. I was the middle child and—" She glanced down at the baby who was now leaning against her, his lids heavy.

"Looks like the naps can't be postponed any longer," Elton said.

"May I come with you to put them down? I can carry Sean."

"Uh, sure," he said agreeably. He picked up the baby girl and led Jane upstairs toward a bedroom wing, pausing at a sun-lightened room. From the doorway, she could see two white cribs at right angles, Jack Be Nimble on one and Little Bo-Peep on the other. The walls were covered in yellow striped wallpaper and decorated with Mother Goose prints.

Elton gestured toward the beds. "That's Sean's bed and over here's Sarah's. He may need changing."

Without any prompting, Jane grabbed a diaper and changed a soggy Sean as Elton observed. Then she moved the boy from the changing table to his crib, hugging him to her as she did so. It was all she could do to leave Sean and his sister and go with Elton downstairs.

"How about some iced tea, Miss Jarrett?" he offered as they reached the bottom landing.

"Fine," she said, and followed him to the kitchen. It was late July and the temperature had soared past one hundred. A glass of tea sounded wonderful about now. Besides, she was anxious to talk to Elton. She had so many questions about the babies, about Greg.

Elton motioned her to a kitchen chair as he filled glass tumblers with ice and poured in tea from a pitcher. "Are you hungry? Sandwich? Piece of cake?"

"No, thanks. Just the tea."

"Terrible hot spell we're having," he said, launching into a lengthy diatribe about Texas summers and the lack of rain this year.

Enough small talk. Jane wished the man would get down to business. She pointedly stared at her watch in hopes of hurrying him along, but he continued to fiddle with his teaspoon.

"What's going on here?" she finally asked in

frustration. Then without letting him speak, she continued, "Why am I meeting with you instead of Mr. Merrifield? Late or not, I made it very clear to him I was coming."

Elton nervously stroked his stubbled chin. "This is hard for Greg. I don't know any other way to say it, ma'am, except to be blunt. Charlotte...that's Mrs. Merrifield, died soon after the babies came. Not from the birthing, but from leukemia. It was her final wish that the boss remarry, that her children have a mother. She made Greg promise to get hitched again and to do it A.S.A.P. That's the reason he placed the ad. Felt he'd put it off as long as he could."

"But why an advertisement? Surely there are women here who are available."

Elton smiled. "Oh, there are women." He chuckled to himself. "Lordy, yes. But according to Greg, none of them would do. That's why I encouraged him to place the ad—told him if he was going to be so persnickety, he'd just have to look farther afield."

"The ad was your idea?"

"Yep. Can't say Greg was all that enthusiastic. Can't say he's enthusiastic even now." Elton met Jane's eyes head-on. "It'll be up to you to convince him otherwise. So, are you interested in trying?"

Jane hesitated as she reflected back to the irritating, but intriguing man she'd talked with. Then her mind drifted to those two darling babies. In the blink of an eye, she'd fallen in love with them. Would it be possible to love their father, too, for him to love her? That was the gamble. She took a deep breath. What was life anyway if not a series of gambles?

"I'm interested...most definitely interested. When can I talk to Mr. Merrifield?"

Elton rubbed his chin again. "Uh, we may have a slight hitch. Please don't take offense, but I'm afraid the boss can't see you looking like you do."

Jane was mystified. "What's wrong with the way I look?"

"You're an awful pretty woman, Miss Jarrett, but way too glamorous, too citified, to fit in around here. Greg'll say you belong somewhere 'uptown,' somewhere like New York or San Francisco—or Dallas. Not Martinsville."

Now Jane wasn't just mystified, she was astonished. "Are you saying he'll hold my appearance against me?"

Elton shrugged a reluctant yes. "I consider myself a good judge of character, ma'am—"

"Call me Jane."

"...Jane. And I have a hunch you'd not only be good at mothering, but good for Greg, too. Only he won't see that—not at first anyway. Not when he gets a gander at you. So what I'm saying is I don't want to hand him an excuse not to give you the benefit of the doubt."

She'd taken such pains with her appearance today; obviously it would have been better if she'd thrown on a pair of old shorts and pulled her hair back with an elastic band—easier, too.

If it weren't for Sean and Sarah, Jane might have turned tail and ran from such stupidity. She'd suffered enough rejection lately and was reluctant to open herself up to more. But her dander was up. *Too glamorous indeed!* She rose, eyes blazing. "That can be remedied. I assure you I can be as unglamorous as the next person."

"I doubt that," Elton said with a smile.

She shot him a withering glare. "All I need are a few hours, then I want to meet with Mr. Merrifield in person."

"A determined lady like you, maybe you should at that," Elton agreed. The smile developed into a deep grin. "How about tomorrow morning? I'll make sure the boss is here."

Eyeing herself in the mirror of the small motel in Pampa where she'd stayed the night, Jane gave herself a thumbs-up. Yes, she'd attained the desired metamorphosis. The loose-fitting skirt and blouse she wore came from the racks of a local discount store and their olive cast couldn't have been less complimentary to her ivory skin. She'd traded her contact lens for eyeglasses, fashioned her long sable brown hair into a tight bun and omitted all makeup except sunblock and lip gloss. Time to meet Greg Merrifield.

Settling behind the steering wheel, Jane stared out through the windshield at the beckoning highway and wondered whether she was making the biggest goof of her life pursuing this course.

A year ago she'd have ridiculed the prospect of marrying a man she'd never met...called it unthinkable. But a year ago she hadn't passed her thirty-third birthday, a year ago she *was* married, and a year ago... Would she ever accept the fact that she'd never be pregnant, never have a child growing inside her, never be a...

That doesn't have to happen. A golden opportunity is right before me. She could still become a mother. She'd found the perfect children, children she could love unconditionally. Maybe Sean and Sarah hadn't been carried under her heart, but they'd won an instant place in it. All she had to do was win over their father. She switched on the car engine and pulled out of the motel parking lot, her resolve restored. The rising sun was tinting the clouds a glorious salmon pink. It was a good omen—she just knew it.

"So you're finally here," Greg said, hoping his voice sounded convincingly indignant. He couldn't let Elton's glowing comments about Jane Jarrett being genuine mom material affect his judgment. Yet the way she was staring adoringly at Sean in his high chair almost got to Greg. Some women would be disgusted with his son's fruit-smeared face, but she seemed amused at the boy's efforts to feed himself.

"Yes, I'm finally here," Jane echoed testily. "If you people had decent road signs, I'd have been here right on the dot yesterday as well." She was smarting at the implication of tardiness when *he* wasn't even there, and feeling an urge to lambaste him royally. She might have, too, except the rancher had Sarah propped in the crook of his arm. Her heart melted every time she glanced his way. And it wasn't just the way he held his baby.

Greg Merrifield fulfilled every female's fantasy

about Texas ranchers. Craggy, irregular features and a mass of unruly blond hair gave him an off-kilter sexiness and he possessed a combination of raw power and casual elegance that would seem natural astride a horse or schmoozing at a cocktail party.

Quite a package. Six foot four, imposing physique, muscles honed by ranch labor. For one accustomed to—bored by—male models with their pretty-boy handsomeness and sleek bodies, Greg was a pulse-raising sensation. No wonder those local females were after him. Jane could just hear her sisters, her friends, maybe even her mom, gasping, ''Be still, my heart.'' Jane was having a bit of difficulty keeping her own heart from fluttering.

''You're not exactly what I expected.''

Greg's comment quickly brought her back to earth. ''And what did you expect?'' she asked, trying to suppress her dismay. An A-OK sign from Elton when she'd arrived told her the brown wren makeover passed muster. Now Jane wondered whether she'd erred in listening to the foreman. Her model's looks always opened doors before. *Why did I let a complete stranger talk me into foregoing a winning image?* Nervously she smoothed her skirt.

''Someone more…more…oh, I don't know…'' *Ordinary.* Greg paused, knowing there was no explaining that bit of idiocy to her. He shook his head. Despite his best efforts, he was letting this far-from-ordinary woman undermine his good sense, the same way she had Elton's. Then again, Elton always had been a sucker for a pretty face. Even Nita said so. And Jane Jarrett's face was more than pretty. She wore little makeup, but then she didn't need to gild the lily. She was beautiful as she was, in an understated way, but still beautiful. Her skin was a flawless porcelain, her lips full and sensuous, her blue, blue eyes striking even behind those glasses.

"If there's something wrong with me, I'd like to hear what it is," Jane said. Just as she'd begun to fear, Greg Merrifield wasn't buying into this plain-Jane approach. She'd blown it.

"I didn't mean to insinuate there was anything wrong." *Actually you're about as perfect as it gets.* "Just thinking you'd probably be more comfortable in jeans than dresses. Jeans would make chasing the twins easier, too—" The words brought Greg up short. Here he was talking about Jane Jarrett becoming a part of his family as if it was a real possibility. "At this age they take a lot of chasing," he added hastily.

"I think I'm up to it. And I do own jeans." Apparently she'd misread him. It wasn't going as bad as she'd thought. Except for that way Greg looked at her. As though he could see right to the core of her. Unconsciously she twisted a strand of hair that had come loose from her bun.

The action set Greg's imagination in motion. He could visualize freeing that satiny mane, letting it cascade down her back, across a pillow... *Man, I'm losing it, daydreaming like some overstimulated schoolboy.* He was seeking a mother for Sean and Sarah, not someone to warm his bed. And with Jane, his thoughts kept careening in that direction. This was wrong. All wrong. He needed to extricate himself from her spell before his brain softened into pure mush.

"Listen, I warned you on the phone that this might be a wild-goose chase. Well, now that I've put more thought into it, the more positive I am that I'm not quite ready for such a commitment. I doubt that you are, either, just divorced and all..."

Greg cautioned himself to keep that fact foremost in his mind. From the little he'd gleaned about Jane, Greg guessed she'd been hurt by the breakup of her marriage. Goodness knows, he would have been if it had happened to him and he wouldn't have gotten over it in a few measly months.

What would happen when Jane's hurt subsided? Things might look completely different to her then and her priorities might take a hundred-and-eighty-degree turn. He couldn't chance discovering down the road that, for her, this had been a fleeting impulse, a whim.

The expression on Jane's face warned Greg she was primed to debate her state of readiness. He didn't want a debate. He wanted her to leave, to go before he begged her to stay. Apparently there was no easy way to run this headstrong lady off, short of making her as mad as heck. "After all," he said imperiously, "if you'd really tried, you could've gotten here on time yesterday."

Her hackles rose. "Surely being late—excusably late at that—is not such a big deal." Jane took a deep breath. "At least *I* showed up eventually. *You* were the one who wasn't willing to hang around." She threw in a steely glare for emphasis.

Neither the glare nor the admonishment evoked

any contrition from the rancher. "Precisely. That should tell us something, too."

"How so?"

"Simple. I've changed my mind about wanting a wife."

CHAPTER THREE

"YOU'VE what?"

The babies jumped. Greg glowered. And Jane immediately regretted raising her voice.

"I've changed my mind about wanting a wife."

"But you can't do that."

"Sure I can. Or is mind changing only a female prerogative?" One eyebrow arched.

"We had an agreement," Jane answered between clenched teeth. "You owe me a fair—"

"I don't owe you a thing, lady," Greg said crossly, annoyed that Jane was forcing the issue. Since meeting her, his second thoughts about remarriage had become third, fourth, fifth thoughts. Jane Jarrett was opening up emotions he didn't want opened. He might be honor bound to fulfill his promise, to get Sean and Sarah a mother, but Greg didn't plan to engage his heart in the process. And that's precisely what could happen with Jane.

"But you let me come out here, indicated—"

Both eyebrows moved, shifting together in a forbidding frown and stopping her in midsentence. "So I did, and naturally I'll reimburse you for the airfare and inconvenience." He stood up, strode to the adjoining family room and set Sarah into the playpen, then came back to the kitchen, where Jane was in the process of cleaning peaches off Sean's grubby little face. Taking the cloth from her, he finished washing the child and carried him to join his sister, disappearing momentarily. When he returned, his hand held a check. "To compensate you for your trouble and expenses," he said giving it to Jane.

"Your money's not what I want." She crushed the check into a ball. "I want—" She had to catch herself before she cried out "you." A ludicrous notion considering Greg's attitude. Ludicrous...but with an element of truth, too. Jane didn't exactly believe in love at first sight, but she did believe in attraction. And Greg Merrifield was attracting her like a powerful magnet. Add to that the bonus of his children and...

"How can you know what you want?" he accused. "I wager you didn't think through all the consequences of marrying a stranger any more than I did. Once you do, believe me, you'll reach the same conclusion I have."

"The conclusion that *you* don't want a wife?"

"That, too," he said, pulling out a chair and sitting down across from her. "But what I really meant was that you'll decide it's too soon for another husband."

Jane could feel her irritation rising at the way he was analyzing her thought processes as though he had the gift of insight. "Isn't that my call, not yours?"

"Okay, then, how about the fact you'd be burning all your bridges by moving halfway across Texas. Surely you have a job, friends, you would be giving up if you settled in Martinsville."

"Haven't you heard?—there are all sorts of

things for keeping in touch...phones, planes, E-mail. And as for my career, well I'm prepared for a change there, too. I—'' Jane stopped. She was about to tell Greg she was a displaced model, then reconsidered. No need giving him another reason to boot her out the door. What she'd witnessed so far didn't suggest a man who'd relish a professional model as caretaker for his children.

She'd worked hard and valued what she'd achieved, but many considered posing for a camera a frivolous career for frivolous people. Greg might be one of those many. ''I'm in advertising—'' Jane improvised, deliberately vague.

''Is that what you were doing in Amarillo?'' he interrupted.

''Yes. A...a special campaign for a cosmetics company. A group of us were there putting together a holiday promotion.'' Jane was staying as close to the truth as possible, all the while suspecting she'd pay for her sins of omission when Greg discovered the whole story.

She'd cross that bridge later. If she and Greg ever came to a meeting of the minds, she'd wait till the time was right—when she was officially established as the new mistress of the Circle G, wife to Greg and mother to the twins—before spilling the tale of her past career. Then it would be too late for him to have another change of heart. Like it or not, he'd be stuck with her.

For the present, all she had to do was penetrate that thick Merrifield skull.

''So you're on vacation this week?'' he asked.

''Well, actually, I go from project to project,''

Jane hedged. "At the present, I'm fresh out of assignments."

"No husband, no 'assignments.' You're fancy-free. How convenient."

"Boss..." Elton warned. He'd been standing in the corner nursing a cup of coffee and monitoring their conversation like an overzealous chaperon.

Greg shot a glare Elton's way. "How about making another pot of coffee since drinking it seems to be your major activity this morning."

Elton glared back but set his cup down and went over to the coffeemaker.

So I'm overdoing the sarcasm. Greg couldn't help it. Jane Jarrett was too threatening. He didn't like the way she made him feel, the way she sent his pulse accelerating when she cast her eyes up at him from under those long silky eyelashes, or caused his temperature to rise when she unleashed one of those captivating smiles.

The only safe path was to put distance between him and the pushy Miss Jarrett. And to do it pronto. "I'm sorry, but nothing you've said has altered my position."

"And that's that? You just decide unilaterally that a marriage is impractical?"

"Let's just say I've come to my senses sooner than you. But you'll see...there are just too many complications. You might as well save us both a lot of consternation and be on your way." He stood up.

Jane remained seated. "But what about Sean and Sarah?"

The beam of a proud father mellowed Greg's features for an instant before his face hardened. He sat back down at the kitchen table, then took both her hands in his. "Look, Jane, there's more to it than admiring a couple of cute kids. You haven't thought about the fact you'd be setting yourself up for a lot of hard work, for years of sacrifice. We're talking lifetime commitment here."

Jane pulled her hands free. "Give me a break. I didn't march into this with blinders on. I know children are demanding, but I believe the rewards are worth it. Naturally I realize I'll…everyone…will need to do a lot of adjusting and—"

"But not as much as you would," he interjected. "It'd be hard for someone from Dalhart or Pampa to pull up roots and live out here, much less someone from a big city like Dallas.

"We're miles from the nearest beauty salon," Greg continued, "and the main recreation is a Saturday night dance at the veterans' hall in Martinsville. Shopping's mainly confined to Franklin Brothers Feed Store and a couple of grocers—and when I say grocers, I don't mean the supermarkets you're used to. We listen to country music instead of that classical stuff and prefer chicken fried steak to that fancy-pants nouvelle cuisine."

"Sounds like we've got something in common, then. I think country music's terrific and chicken fried steak's one of my favorite foods."

"Well, that's a start," Elton interjected.

Greg halted, but only for a second. Paying no heed to either one of them, he continued his litany. "If you want a new dress, you have to go to Pampa, where you're probably aware there's no Neiman-Marcus. The ranch is unbearably hot in the summer and blustery cold in the winter—occasionally snowed-in, in fact.''

''You *do* make it sound appealing,'' Jane said flippantly, helping herself to a glass of orange juice from a pitcher on the table.

''That's the way it is.''

''I'll adapt.'' She sipped her juice, her eyes carefully watching his reaction over the rim of her glass. Greg shook his head, serving notice that her ability to adapt wasn't within the realm of possibility.

Seeing that Greg was tuning her out, Elton repeated Jane's comment. ''She'll adapt, Greg.''

''Miss Jarrett wouldn't be happy here,'' Greg declared, rebutting Elton's plea and wishing his foreman would mind his own business for a change. ''The Circle G is too remote and Martinsville isn't Dallas.''

''Gee, I wish I'd known that before I came all the way out here,'' Jane noted sarcastically. Greg Merrifield must have watched too many episodes of the old television show ''Dallas.'' Did he think everyone there was a clone of the Ewings—owning mansions, sporting designer clothes and spending their evenings bed-hopping or skipping from one society bash to another? He had to know better. Searching for excuses, that's what he was about. Jane was even more nettled that Merrifield directed his comments about her to the foreman as if she weren't there.

''I'm serious, Miss Jarrett,'' he said, turning back

to her. "I'm trying to point out some of the hurdles you'd face."

"No, you're trying to discourage me. And I can't understand why. But I bet you chose that course before I ever got here. Why did you let me bother when you never really planned to give me a chance?"

"She's right, Greg," Elton chimed in. "The little lady's come a long way. You oughta hear her out before deciding this can't work. She deserves that much."

Greg scowled at Elton, then at her.

Five-ten in her stocking feet, Jane was tall even next to a man of Greg's stature. "*Little* lady, my foot," he was probably saying to himself.

Nonetheless, Elton's strong support momentarily revived her hopes and she vowed to take full advantage of this opportunity. "All I've wanted is for you to be openminded about this."

"Yeah, Greg, openminded," Elton echoed. "Ask her some questions at least."

"I don't have time for questions today," Greg said sternly. "I've got things to do."

Jane was certain she'd never met a harder-headed, more stubborn man in her life. He might not want a wife, now or ever. Well she wasn't so darn sure she wanted him for a husband, either. So why was she continuing to plead her case? It was the babies that were drawing her, she rationalized. If it weren't for them, she'd bolt from here so fast Greg would think a Texas twister had blown through.

"Sounds like copping out to me," she complained, her temper simmering, threatening to erupt. "Of course, what you really mean is that you won't *take* time. Odd, since you *are* the one who advertised for a wife—remember?"

Greg's shoulders shifted in an exaggerated droop. "Who's going to let me forget?"

"Not me." Elton popped up.

"Okay, okay. It's evident there'll be no peace if I don't interview the 'little lady.'" Greg filled a coffee mug, offering it to Jane.

His capitulation was unexpected—and disarming. Was Greg actually reconsidering, or merely pacifying Elton? Curiosity prompted Jane to tamp down any remnants of temper until she found out. She smiled and accepted the coffee.

Greg propped a hip against the counter. "So you're not tied to your job. Do you have hobbies, other things, to keep you busy?" He grinned slyly at Jane. "When you're not answering ads or husband hunting, that is."

That did it. So much for hoping Greg had changed his spots. Babies aside, no way was she going to suffer this galoot's contrariness for another second. She stood, hands pressed on the table as she leaned in Greg's direction. "I'd hoped you'd decided to be agreeable, but obviously—"

"I don't think Greg meant that the way it sounded," Elton interrupted.

Jane rolled her eyes in disbelief.

He turned to Greg. "Tell her you weren't insinuating anything bad."

"The heck he wasn't," Jane countered.

Greg didn't bother to retract the taunt.

"Now come on you two," Elton said. "This isn't the way for grown-ups to go about getting acquainted. Think about the babies."

The babies. Magic words. If she gave in to her urge to flee, they'd be lost to her forever. Jane wanted those babies. She saw the expression on Greg's face alter too. But just for a moment.

"Elton, I thought you had some repairs to oversee at the corral." Greg's voice had an unmistakable edge that said Elton was skating on thin ice.

Although clearly skeptical of their resolving matters without him, Elton grudgingly nodded. "Guess I do. See you later, Miss Jarrett?" The question was aimed at Greg rather than Jane.

Nevertheless, Jane took the initiative to respond, "Maybe. Who knows?"

As soon as Elton was out the door, she said to Greg, "And will I? See him again, I mean."

"If Elton has his way," Greg replied noncommittally. "You've really charmed him. And he says you're good with the children. What little I've seen possibly proves him right."

Jane couldn't believe her ears. Actual words of praise. "They're very dear," she said. "But I've already told you that."

"Naturally, as their father, I totally agree. Still I'm stumped about why you're here in the first place, why you're so damn persistent." Greg furrowed his forehead and ran fingers through his mass of hair. "You're not a bad-looking woman. Surely you don't have to resort to gimmicks to land a husband."

"The way you felt it necessary to use a gimmick to locate a wife?"

"Well—"

"A gimmick that got results, too. Before your very eyes is a potential candidate, and you shouldn't cut her loose so easily. Who can guess when the next one might come along? Perhaps never."

"I should be so lucky," he muttered.

Jane had to suppress a smile. You'd think Greg Merrifield was some wild mustang bucking against being saddled. Which made absolutely no sense. He'd already been married, had— *Is that the reason for his resistance? Can he simply not bear the thought of bringing another woman into his life?*

"Actually I've been concentrating on the children," she said, shaking off her qualms and hoping to counteract his apprehension of her as a huntress. "I really hadn't pictured this as a husband-finding mission."

"The ad did say 'wife' as well as 'mother.'" He appeared scornful of her claim that she was focusing on the latter.

"I realize that—" To Jane's relief, whimpers from the playpen rescued her from finishing the sentence. She had no notion of what to say anyway. This was the awkward part of the arrangement, discussing a relationship with someone she'd known mere hours. The knowledge that thousands of marriages throughout history had been arranged by intermediaries, with little or no contact between the principals, didn't make Jane any more comfortable.

Along with Greg, she rose and went to the den,

each of them picking up a baby, and both apparently willing to drop the subject of their future for now.

"Sarah needs a fresh diaper," she said.

"Might as well take them up for their naps." Greg nuzzled his son's soft, fat neck. The baby's scrunched fists were rubbing his eyes.

Once the two children were changed and settled down, Jane and Greg went back to the large kitchen, which seemed to serve as a gathering room. They sat at the table again, each with a fresh cup of coffee in hand.

"Do you and Elton take care of the twins on your own?" Jane asked.

"Nah. Helga, our cook and housekeeper, does the lion's share when I'm working. And Elton... well he's more of a grandpa to them."

"Where is Helga?"

"She had to take a few days off this week. Her husband is sick."

"I could pitch in until she returns," Jane offered. "Give us a chance to get to know each other better."

He eyed her warily. "Aggressive, aren't you?"

"One of us has to be."

"Maybe. But I have the distinct impression you're expecting more from this than I'm willing to give. If you've got some big illusion that the love match of the century is going to come from a newspaper ad, then—"

"Is that what you're afraid of? That I'll expect your love? Whatever led you to that conclusion?" Jane's heart thudded uncomfortably. Greg

Merrifield had read her all too well. Maybe she shouldn't be weaving dream castles, but simply because she'd had one rotten marriage didn't mean she couldn't wish an alliance with Greg to be different. To accept that she could never be happily married again would be the ultimate defeat.

"It's not fear, it's reality. I received enough letters from women like you to give me insight into the way a woman thinks. Life isn't a romance novel, honey. It's hard and tough, and happy endings aren't guaranteed. So why don't you grab your purse and go home like I suggested. Maybe in a couple of weeks we can put this fiasco behind us."

"That's beginning to sound like a great idea," Jane said, not bothering to control the bite in her voice. "You have no intention of keeping your promise to Charlotte anyway."

Knowing she had crossed the line, Jane fully expected her comment to cause a stir. And she got one. Greg's reaction was immediate in the crimson flush coloring his face and the ominous darkening of his brown eyes. "Someone's got a big mouth," he barked. "Hellfire, did Elton also tell you what style of underwear I wear and mention the scar on my behind, too?"

Greg's laserlike stare pinned her with a force strong enough to shatter diamonds. "Let's get one thing straight right now," he dictated. "Whatever has occurred between *us,* my relationship with Charlotte and any promises I made to her are none of your concern!"

"I beg to differ," Jane snapped back. "That promise is the only reason I'm here and you know it. Despite all your carrying-on about not being ready, etcetera, etcetera, you impress me as a man who takes promises seriously. You didn't advertise because you were Mr. Lonely Hearts. You were fulfilling a pledge, a pledge I want to help you keep.''

She could see him blanch at her remark and she guessed that Greg Merrifield, as glum as he might be about the prospect, probably would re-marry…eventually. After all, he had sworn to do so. The problem was if Jane failed to seize this opportunity, the bride would be someone else, the mother to Sean and Sarah would be someone else. Considering Greg's contentious posturing, that might be to her benefit, but an inner part of her knew she didn't want it to happen. Jane saw his contentiousness as a defense mechanism and she didn't want to give up on the real man hidden behind it.

Time was of the essence, Jane realized. Not only for Greg, but for her, too. She couldn't afford to wait indefinitely. Her agenda was open at the present, but soon she'd have to make decisions regarding her future. If she took too long a sabbatical from modeling, she might have difficulty ever working as one again. Clearly she needed to prod this reluctant suitor along.

''Perhaps if I told you more about myself,'' she volunteered.

Greg's shrug conveyed his lack of enthusiasm. He took a swallow of coffee and focused straight ahead.

''Okay, for starters,'' she said, undeterred, ''I'm

a Dallas native, born, raised, grade school, high school, attended college at the University of Dallas—"

"I don't need a day-by-day autobiography," he groused, standing up and carrying his cup to the sink.

Jane heaved a sigh of disappointment. Was there nothing she could do to generate a spark?

"I've already told you I want to be a mother. And those two are so special."

"So you keep saying. What you haven't explained is why you're so dead set on this," he said.

"For years now..." she began, seeing it as crucial that she clarify her reasons. Obviously she hadn't managed to so far. "For years, I've wanted a family...a family of my own. One that includes children. As much as I adore my nieces and nephews, I want more than the role of indulgent maiden aunt. Recently I found out I can't have children. I won't bore you with the medical details, but suffice it to say, it's fact, not supposition."

"I see. And you've ruled out adoption?"

"That usually takes a couple of years...longer for a single person. I'm not sure I want to forfeit all those years, now that I've found two perfectly wonderful babies with no mother, and a father with a promise to keep." She met his gaze head-on. "I can make your life better, you know."

"Can you?" Greg lashed out. He couldn't take much more of this, couldn't allow this woman to get under his skin any more than she already had. "I've said it before and I'll say it again, I don't want a wife. I don't want *you*, Miss Jarrett." Even as the words left his lips, Greg knew he was lying. He wanted her something awful and he hated the desire within him—desire that could cloud his thinking if he let it.

The wounded expression on her face told him the message had hit home. She sat there for long moments, every tick of the wall clock making him feel more like the cretinous jerk he'd been.

Jane stared at Greg Merrifield unseeingly, and realized she was beaten. She'd tried cajoling, humoring, altering her appearance, practically begged—desperate tactics aimed at influencing him. And what good had it done? Even if he did ultimately cave in, what kind of relationship dared she hope for when he was barely civil to her?

It wasn't as if she were asking for the same kind of love and devotion he'd shown his late wife. Yet he *could* love again. It might take a while, but it could happen. If only he'd deign to try. It seemed, however, Greg Merrifield would rather feel sorry for himself than entertain possibilities of a second chance.

She could have followed that same route. After her failed marriage, it would have been easy to become the pessimist, to decide that love was not in the cards for her, but Jane was determined to rise above such fatalism. And she thought she'd found a way, by sharing Greg Merrifield's future, his children. Apparently that was not to be. Apparently there was never to be room in Greg's heart or his life for anyone else.

As she contemplated saying farewell, a huge lump formed in Jane's throat. *Do not cry,* she ordered herself. *You've made fool enough of yourself already.* Jane refused to grovel any longer. Her sole objective at the moment was to get out of here without further embarrassment.

Anger replacing defeat, she stood up and stared down at the husband who might have been. "Well, it's a good thing you don't want *me,* Mr. Merrifield, because I don't want a cynical...cynical...*cowboy* for a husband. I wouldn't have you if you came served on a silver platter with an apple in your mouth."

Haughtily Jane traipsed to the hall for her purse and strode purposefully out to her car. Not until the Circle G ranch house was out of sight did the hot tears start to course down her cheeks.

CHAPTER FOUR

"Now you've gone and done it!"

Jane had just driven away in a cloud of dust when Elton bounded up the porch steps. "That was a nice woman and she'd be a good mama for those babies, but you treated her like some moocher begging for a handout. The fix you're in isn't Miss Jarrett's fault, you know. You oughta be ashamed of yourself for behaving like that." Elton rested a foot atop one of the porch chairs and removed a package of cigarettes from his pocket.

"I keep reminding you those things are poison," Greg griped, seizing the excuse to divert Elton's attention.

"And I keep reminding you about the promise you made to Charlotte," the foreman retorted. "Doesn't seem like either of us listens too good." Defiantly he struck a match off the bottom of his boot and lit the cigarette. "Well, what do you intend to do now?"

Greg shrugged. He didn't have the slightest idea. Elton was right—he'd behaved abominably around Jane Jarrett, and was embarrassed just to think about it. If he could, he'd play the whole scene again. Trouble was, even if he could repeat the meeting with her, he doubted whether he'd do anything differently. He might admit he hadn't treated the woman fairly, but in a way she was the one who'd provoked his actions by pushing him into a corner where antagonism was his only escape. Still, that didn't relieve his feeling lower than a snake.

Elton was puffing on his cigarette, plainly contemplating his next volley when the sound of an engine captured his and Greg's attention. A black Jeep approached the house. Helga's Jeep. Although grateful he'd been rescued from further criticism, Greg also realized he was disappointed that it was his housekeeper, rather than Jane returning.

Helga stayed only a few minutes, just long enough to deliver a tearful resignation and to see the babies again. A half hour later the two men were still on the front porch, both reeling from her sad news and its consequences. Helga's husband Rafe needed a bypass operation so she wouldn't be able to work again for some time, if ever.

"Hate to say I told you so," Elton said.

"Then don't," Greg answered with the grumpiness of a man who has his back against the wall. How could he possibly run the ranch without someone to tend the children during the day?

"Can't help it. If you'd been nicer to Miss Jarrett, you wouldn't be in such a pickle. You *really* need her now." Elton crushed out one cigarette, then immediately lit another.

"Keep up that nasty habit and you'll be in the same condition as Rafe and I'll be pacing some hospital corridor worrying about *you* making it through heart surgery."

"I hate it when you're right," Elton said, snuffing out the cigarette. "I need to give up these danged coffin nails." He patted Greg on the arm.

"Nita can pitch in with the twins for now, but I hope you'll reconsider Miss Jarrett. A new mama's the best way to end this crisis."

"Oh, sure. The lady would be real impressed to know that since my housekeeper quit, I'm willing to marry her after all. Get serious, Elton."

"She was crazy about those babies, probably crazy enough to overlook being manipulated."

Greg shook his head. "Let it be, okay? Give your missus a call and ask her if she'll come over for a few days until I figure out what to do."

"You know she will. I'll go pick her up."

"Thanks. After you fetch Nita, I need to get back to work. I suggest you do the same."

"Yes, sir, boss sir." Elton snapped to attention, his annoyance evident.

Greg realized how high-handed he'd sounded. "You know I didn't mean it like that." He clasped the older man on the shoulder. "And about Miss Jarrett...I'm sorry I was such an—"

"Save your breath." Elton interrupted. "She's the one you should be telling, not me." He trotted toward his pickup truck before Greg had a chance to respond.

For the next two days Elton's words preyed on Greg's mind. He couldn't expect Jane to rescue him from the loss of Helga, but he still owed her an apology. Only thing was, he didn't particularly enjoy eating crow. *So who does like fessing up to a wrong? Call the woman and tell her you're sorry so you can get on with your life.* Knowing he wouldn't be able to get Jane off his mind until he did just that, Greg reluctantly dialed her number that evening.

"Hello, this is Greg Merr—"

She slammed down the receiver, fervently hoping the bang punctured his eardrum. *How dare he call! There's nothing he can say that I need to hear.*

In the days since her return from the Circle G, Jane had been hanging around her condominium, more depressed than she'd been before that ridiculous scheme had enveloped her and altered her life. Her visions of home and family had been unspecific, amorphous, until she met Greg Merrifield and his children. But once she embarked on that ill-fated trip, the visions became real, with actual people in them. The children she desired were Sean and Sarah. The husband—

The telephone rang once more and this time Jane checked her caller identification. She could see it was Greg. What was he up to anyway? Hadn't he said way too much already? Well, she wasn't going to talk to him. Or any other man. As of this week Jane had sworn off men. Especially this one. She wasn't about to put herself through the ordeal of another disagreeable conversation with him. The telephone kept ringing until the answering machine started.

"I know you're there and you might as well pick up," she heard Greg bark. "I plan to keep on calling until you answer, even if it takes all night and half the day tomorrow."

Jane contemplated yanking the telephone plug from the outlet, but changed her mind. It might discourage him this time, but she couldn't keep the phone unplugged forever. With Greg more persistent than a telemarketer on commission, she might as well talk to him and get it over with. She grabbed the receiver. "What do you want?" she demanded.

"Well, uh…"

"Uh what?" She wasn't about to fall for any shy, tongue-tied act. Jane knew better. Greg was about as shy and tongue-tied as a politician.

"You're not making this easy on a guy."

"And why should I? You didn't exactly treat me with kid gloves. Listen, Merrifield, I'm out of your life just like you wanted. Now leave me alone."

"I had that coming," Greg said. "But I didn't call to hound you. I just wanted to explain…to tell you…I feel bad about the way our meeting went."

"Oh, really? Pity you didn't think of that before you deliberately sabotaged it."

"I owe you an apology," he continued. "Let me—"

"Don't bother trying to salve your conscience," she said. "It's too late." She slammed down the receiver again, unwelcome tears streaming down her face. She'd never forgive him for raising her hopes, then dashing them.

Greg started to dial a third time, but stopped before he'd punched in all the numbers. He was pretty sure the attempt would be useless anyway. Jane wasn't in what you'd call a reasonable mood. Why should he give a flip anyway? He'd tried to make amends. If she wanted to hold a grudge that was her problem.

He climbed the stairs to look in on the twins. Sound asleep. Elton and Nita had gone home for the day and the house was silent. Unbearably so. Yet for the first time in months, the silence didn't cause Greg's thoughts to go inward, to focus on the changes the previous year had wrought. Instead they gravitated to his telephone conversation with Jane. The more he reflected on her stubbornness, the madder he got.

It bugged him that she wouldn't listen. All he'd wanted to do was take responsibility for his bad manners, explain that nothing he'd said or did was her fault. That was it. He only rang because he didn't like feeling shamefaced.

Well, the lady's going to receive a proper apology whether she wants one or not. As soon as he could get away, he'd ask Elton and Nita to stay overnight with the babies while he made a fast trip to Dallas. Until he got Jane Jarrett out of his system, he'd never be able to concentrate on more essential tasks, like finding a new housekeeper. He poured two fingers of bourbon from a decanter on a side bar and slowly sipped the potent liquid while he formulated a plan. The thing to do was just appear on her doorstep and express his regrets. Then he'd be done with the woman.

When the doorbell rang early the next Wednesday evening Jane was irritated. Company was not on her docket. Still keeping to herself, she was using tonight for a beauty redo. Her oil-treated hair was wrapped in a towel and she'd just peeled the cucumber masque from her face. She looked a mess.

Warily she slipped on her glasses and made her way to the door. She stared through the peephole, hoping it was someone she could readily ignore—like a solicitor. *It couldn't be...but it was—Greg Merrifield!* The last person on earth she expected to see. More astonishingly, he carried a lavish bouquet of flowers.

As she hesitated, the bell rang again. "I know you're in there," he shouted through the door. "I can hear music. Are you going to open up or shall I deliver my sentiments out here in front of God and everybody?"

Jane opened the door and he thrust the flowers into her arms. "Since you wouldn't accept my apology over the phone, I drove down to say it in person. And maybe buy you a drink to make amends," he added.

Jane put a hand to her towel and glanced down at her outfit—faded shorts and a rumpled T-shirt. "As you can see, I'm not prepared to go out. But thanks for the flowers anyway. Apology noted." She started pushing the door closed, but Greg's foot prevented its shutting.

"Go away," she demanded.

"No," he said, applying pressure against the door. "I'm not leaving till I've said all I came to say."

"Oh, all right," Jane huffed. She should have listened to him on the phone and been done with him. Now she had to pay for that lack of foresight. "Come on in. But say your piece fast." Jane stepped back and allowed him entrance into the condo.

"Thanks for the gracious welcome," he drawled, strolling in and making himself at home on the couch without waiting for an invitation to sit down. He took a few moments to look around the large living room. "Nice place. *Very* nice. Definitely the high-rent district. Don't tell me you can afford this on your, ah, flexible...work schedule?"

She dropped the flowers onto a nearby table and stood watching him, her arms crossed defensively. "You didn't come all this way to admire my home. And it couldn't be just to keep insulting me either."

"No...disregard what I said. I simply came to tell you that I accept total blame for...for everything. It was all my fault and it never should have happened."

"And you think your showing up here and declaring that makes me feel better?"

"I hoped it would," he admitted uneasily.

"Well, think again." She'd been morose all week without any way to vent her feelings. Now Greg had unwittingly provided her a handy target. "Since your ad made its way into my life, I've been an emotional Ping-Pong ball—yes, he's willing, no he's not willing. But now I've stopped deceiving myself. You've delivered the message that you want no part of me loud and clear. And let me tell you this, Greg Merrifield, the feeling is mutual. I don't want any part of you, either, and I really sympathize with the woman you decide to marry—if you ever do decide, that is. Now why don't you do us both a favor and go away."

Jane could feel her eyes moisten, and the pain she'd tried to suppress for days bubbled to the surface. *No, don't you dare start bawling.* She couldn't lose her cool in front of him. Never. She snuffled, trying to hold back the tears.

Greg was stunned. He hadn't expected this re-action. Sure, a little anger, maybe, but not this self-deprecation. And were those tears forming in her eyes? *Oh, Jeez.* He'd never been able to handle a woman's crying.

"Uh, look," he finally said, rising to his feet. "You're misunderstanding everything." He crossed the room and took her hand in his. "I wanted to ask for another chance. That's why I'm here—to ask you to come back."

"What? Is this some kind of joke?"

"No, no," he protested. "We just got off on the wrong foot—that's all. You were right about us needing a longer visit from you...a whole week...so everyone can get better acquainted. This isn't the kind of decision that should be made on the spur-of-the-moment, especially with Elton poking his nose in like he was. What do you say?"

Jane was flabbergasted. She'd figured never to hear from Greg Merrifield again. He'd been so ad-amant...and now this about-face. It was too much to comprehend. "This is so unexpected..." she be-gan. The offer was back on the table. How could she ignore it? She had told him she wanted no part of him but that was not completely true. There *was* a very important part she wanted—those babies. *Just the babies?* her conscience nagged. Jane brushed the thought aside and looked up at him. "Are you sure?"

He gazed into her shimmering eyes. "Of course I'm sure. Come as soon as you can."

She snuffled again. "Well then, okay. I'll do it. I can be there on Friday."

When the door closed, Jane ripped the towel from her head and hugged it to her. *This might just work. Sean and Sarah might just become hers after all.* And the specter of a life ahead with the tantalizing but erratic Mr. Merrifield? Well, one thing at a time, she told herself. One thing at a time. For now she had to concentrate on next week.

Greg walked down the front sidewalk toward his minivan. *What on earth did I just do?* He'd come here to make amends, to purge his guilt. But not like this. Flowers, a bit of groveling, a hasty exit. That was the agenda. *What had gone haywire?* The minute those vivid blue eyes started working on him, he'd gotten sidetracked. First a request to have a drink, and then—he still couldn't fathom it himself—an invitation to come back to the Circle G.

He revved the engine and pulled away from the curb. *Elton is going to love this. Probably strain a stomach muscle from all the guffawing.* Well, Elton wasn't going to be privy to the whole story. Greg would never hear the end of it if he confessed to melting over teary eyes and to extending an invitation he never meant to issue. No, he'd just let Elton think his advice about reconsidering Jane had been heeded.

"Déjà vu," Jane said aloud as she turned her BMW into the driveway of the Circle G on Friday morning.

Greg met her on the front steps. "Well, you're

here,'' he observed, stating the obvious, his voice cordial, and at the same time stiff.

Appropriately so, she told herself. This *is* a little awkward. Uncertainly she thrust her hand out to shake his. ''Hello again.''

Elton appeared at the door. ''Miss Jarrett!'' he called out, his expression showing pleasure at seeing her. ''Let me help you with your bags.''

''It's Jane, remember?'' She dropped her keys into his palm.

''Sure thing, Jane.'' Elton hustled to the car and unlatched the trunk.

''Come on in,'' Greg said, opening the leaded-glass door and ushering her inside. ''You must be tired after that long drive. You're earlier than I expected. When did you leave anyway?''

''Yesterday. I drove to Vernon, then stopped to break up my trip. So, no, I'm not tired.''

''Oh…that's good,'' Greg said. He stood facing Jane in the large tiled entry, his discomfort evidenced in the way he was shifting from one foot to another. ''I'd better show you where you'll be sleeping,'' he offered as Elton joined them with Jane's luggage.

Greg carried her suitcases to a spare bedroom next to the nursery. The room was welcoming, sunny with lots of windows, the windowsills decorated with greenery-filled ceramic pots. ''I'll just leave you to get settled,'' Greg said. ''The babies are taking a morning nap but should wake up any minute. If you need anything, Elton or his wife, Nita, will be around.''

Jane started unpacking—jeans and T-shirts suitable to the casual atmosphere at the ranch. With Elton's caution about fitting in still in mind, she'd brought clothing guaranteed to raise no eyebrows. Her designer clothes along with most of her makeup were still back in Dallas.

She'd no sooner finished storing her empty suitcases under the bed when fretful whimpers emanated from the nursery. The babies were stirring. Happily, she rushed to them, and her heart filled to bursting as two smiles greeted her over the tops of their beds.

"Hi, darlings," she cried, lifting them from the beds and plopping them onto the carpet. Arranging blocks and colorful toys within their reach, Jane joined them on the floor. The time passed so quickly that when she looked at her watch, she was shocked to discover it was noon. Her arms holding one baby apiece, she gingerly descended the carpeted steps to the kitchen.

A small, stocky woman with an old-fashioned wraparound apron covering her ample girth was returning a jar of mayonnaise to the refrigerator shelf. She turned and introduced herself when she heard Jane. "I'm Nita Jones. Welcome to the Circle G. And let me lighten your load."

"Hello." Jane smiled at the warm greeting and handed Sean over. "I was playing with the children." She placed Sarah in her high chair.

"I know," Nita answered. "I peeked in on you when I brought the laundry up. You three were getting along so nicely I didn't have the heart to interrupt. Those wee ones are awfully taken with you."

Jane smiled. Sean's and Sarah's quick acceptance made her more confident that returning was the thing to do. "Can I help you?" she asked. Nita was making sandwiches—tuna salad on whole wheat bread.

"If you'll feed the twins, I'll keep on with what I'm doing." She pointed to two matching plates decorated with Beatrix Potter characters.

As Jane spoon-fed mashed sweet potatoes and applesauce, Nita arranged the sandwiches on a big whitestone platter, then filled baby bottles with milk. "It's probably time to wean them, but I told Greg not to rush," she said, handing a bottle to Jane. Nita cuddled Sean while he drank; Sarah was in Jane's arms. Full and happy, the babies were returned to their high chairs and given toys for their amusement.

A few minutes later Greg and Elton wandered in. Lunch was pleasant with the men doing most of the talking and the twins offering diversions by dropping toys for one of the adults to pick up. The meal was almost over when Jane asked about the Circle G housekeeper. "How's Helga's husband? Is he improving?"

Silence. Deafening silence. Then Greg spoke. "Unfortunately, no. His condition was worse than we thought. He needed open-heart surgery and Helga had to quit to take care of him."

"Oh?" Jane could feel the blood rush to her scalp as it suddenly dawned on her why she was back at the Circle G and why Greg was practically choking with politeness toward her. Before, he couldn't bring himself to replace a wife, but losing his housekeeper had apparently cast new light on the matter. "Well," she said with a fake chuckle, "before you offer me the job, I'd better make it clear that I don't do windows."

To her surprise, Greg took her seriously. "I wouldn't expect you to." Then realizing his error, he smiled self-consciously and stood up. "Since everyone's finished, I'll ask you all to pardon me so I can get to town. I have an appointment I couldn't get out of."

"What about dessert?" Nita asked. "It's black-berry cobbler."

"Save me some for later." Greg left the room.

Nita went to the cupboard for more plates. "No cobbler for me, either, hon," Elton said, rising. "Need to go pick up some antibiotics from Doc Pritchett. Got a sick calf on my hands. See you two gals later."

As Nita served their plates, Jane reflected on the Helga situation. Nita couldn't be expected to pitch in indefinitely so Greg was in a bind. He'd made it clear he wasn't ready to remarry. But Helga's quitting deprived him of a dependable babysitter. Perhaps she had been brought here as a stop gap rather than to give both of them the chance to assess whether a future together was a real possibility.

He'd done a first-rate con job getting her back to the ranch and it would be interesting to see how much diplomacy he'd employ to pitch his case to her. Jane didn't know whether to be grateful for this turn of events or furious that she was being used in such flagrant fashion. She had to acknowledge, however, that for the second time fate had stepped in to throw them together.

Over cups of coffee in the family room, Nita showed Jane pictures of the Merrifield family in happier times and related loving stories of Charlotte Merrifield. "She was a pretty thing, with soft green eyes. Little, though. More'n a foot shorter than Greg, but what was there was all heart. As sweet a girl as you'd ever meet. You'd have liked her. Everybody did."

Holding an album retrieved from a nearby bookcase, Jane could see for herself the young woman Nita was talking about.

Jane knew Nita's reminiscing was well-meaning, that she was purposely providing Jane some background information, but that didn't keep Jane from comparing herself to Charlotte with her angel face and golden hair. Jane's face was more in keeping with today's models: exotic rather than angelic, and her own tresses were the same deep shade as the chestnut mare she'd seen in the ranch corral. And while Charlotte was tiny, Jane—as Elton would have put it—was "a mite larger." Jane had always scoffed at women who were all-consumed with beauty, tending to take her own for granted. But at the moment, she couldn't prevent a twinge of envy.

The rest of the day was spent caring for the babies with Nita providing input on their day-to-day routine. Before leaving, Nita cooked a scrumptious dinner, a hearty pot roast and yeasty cloverleaf rolls. The knot in Jane's stomach kept her from enjoying it, though. The babies were already tucked in bed and she and Greg were eating alone, she filled with nervous anticipation.

But rather than explore the subject of a possible union, Greg seemed content to make small talk about the ranch. "We run several hundred head and grow corn and wheat. Not a big operation by Texas standards. But it keeps a roof over our heads."

All well and good, Jane wanted to say. *But I'd rather talk about us.*

"Then again," Greg drawled, "maybe not as fine a roof as you're used to. I'll have to admit that condo of yours is pretty swanky."

She picked at her dinner, avoiding his gaze and avoiding answering. He was fishing for information, obviously curious about how she could manage the cost of such a posh residence. Well, she wasn't going to give him the whole truth about her modeling, her finances, until he had a right to know. So far he had no rights.

"Whether you realize it or not, you'd be a lot happier back there," he said.

"And you're an authority on happiness?" she snapped back irritatedly.

"Once I was."

There was a catch in Greg's voice that made Jane feel chastened. "Sorry," she said.

"Sorry…" Greg repeated. "I've heard that more times than I can count. My mother's favorite saying was 'Laugh and the world laughs with you. Weep and you weep alone.' I didn't weep alone when Charlotte died, many others also shed tears. But after a while I was the only one still crying. My crying's over now, but I suspect yours isn't. They tell me divorce is a lot like death and if so, then seven months hardly seems long enough to mourn.''

Jane felt a surge of tenderness at Greg's unexpected openness. Honest conversation like this could go a long way to forging a relationship. However, his reasoning about her need for more mourning was misguided.

''Some of what you say is true,'' she admitted, ''but just because my divorce was recent, doesn't mean the marriage wasn't in trouble long before.''

''In trouble and officially over are two different critters. There's hope with the first. I still think you're rushing things, that you've come out here half-cocked. That's why I'm cautioning you not to disrupt your life and end up miserable.''

Jane's tender feelings quickly faded. His predicament with Helga notwithstanding, it appeared they were back to square one. She was tired of him using *her* as an excuse for his foot-dragging. It seemed they were getting nowhere. ''Are you *ever-so-diplomatically* telling me to pack up and head home?''

He studied her across the table and Jane expected him to say that's exactly what he had in mind. But he didn't. ''Of course not. Don't get your feathers ruffled,'' he chided before touching his mouth with his napkin and glancing at his watch. ''It's eight o'clock. How about a little television?''

Television wasn't what she had in mind—far from it. She was tempted to press the issue, to say, ''Forget about me and my divorce and tell me more about you—not the ranch, not the crops...just you.'' But he was signaling a reluctance to talk further. Jane decided to bide her time and, as he suggested, "not get her feathers ruffled."

The next few days were much the same, with Jane tending to the children and becoming familiar with the ranch house. As Greg had said, the Circle G wasn't Dallas. To Jane that was a plus. She'd grown tired of the Metroplex rat race—the traffic, the crowds—and the idea of moving away to a placid setting was appealing. Sure, she'd want to go home, keep close ties with her family, but Jane saw a satisfying change of pace here and the possibility of true happiness. If only Greg would meet her halfway.

She'd been at the ranch four days now and had eased into a routine. Coffee, cereal and juice on arising, followed by breakfast for the twins, then dressing—herself and them. She'd play with the babies, read simple stories and sing lullabies. When Sean and Sarah didn't need her, Jane would take walks around the grounds or assist Nita with meals and housework. The two women had established an easy friendship and Nita filled a need for female companionship while Jane experimented with this dramatic transition from city living to ranch life.

Evenings were spent with Greg. The hours together provided Jane a view of what marriage to him could be like. He was a wonderful father, easygoing, openly demonstrative, his affection for the twins obviously reciprocated. Sarah said "Da Da" constantly, and the moment Greg appeared in a room, both babies squealed and raised their arms to be lifted into a giant embrace.

And Greg could be entertaining to be around for

grown people, too. During suppers alone with him, she'd discovered a quick wit and a droll sense of humor. They talked about books and movies and television, his preferences surprisingly similar to hers. But there'd been no discussion of marriage. That was why she was here after all. She'd waited long enough for Greg to make a move. It was time for action.

Supper was over, the twins in bed, and Greg in front of the television, when Jane broached the topic. "Have you given any more thought to...to us?"

Greg tried not to wince. He'd barely been able to keep his mind on anything else. Elton and a group of ranch hands had been razzing him just this morning. He'd been deep in thought about Jane instead of watching where he was going and stepped right in a pile of horse manure. No two ways about it, his mind was not on ranching.

This couldn't go on—Jane staying at the Circle G. Yet Greg didn't want it to end, either. It felt good having her waiting when he got home in the evening, nice having someone to talk to whose vocabulary extended beyond a few words. Sean and Sarah were adorable, but limited in the conversation department.

He looked at Jane and realized he'd already grown accustomed to her being around, that he was going to have a void to fill when she left. It would be so natural to move closer, to pull her into his arms. Greg couldn't let that happen. Once he did, he'd be a goner for sure, his heart no longer his.

Greg could think of a hundred things that could

go wrong, beginning with Jane deciding that the arrangement wasn't to her liking. After the novelty wore off, she could hate it here—miss working, miss her friends, miss the hubbub. She could become sulky, solemn. Or she could just leave, abandon him and the kids. Or she could get sick...

Jane had to go. He'd lament her absence, yes, but at least with her gone, he'd be protecting himself and the twins from possible hurt. There'd been enough hurt already. "We'll talk tomorrow," he told her, before his grim musings could sink any lower.

Picking up the remote control and changing the channel, he signaled the end to conversation. Then, against his better judgment, he took her hand. Right now he craved her touch. It had been so long since he'd felt a woman's warmth. But this would be the last time—the only time.

Several hours had passed since she'd gone to bed and Jane was in deep slumber when the cry startled her. She jumped up and rushed next door, worried that the baby had been wailing unheard for some time. Sean was sitting up and sobbing, his distressed face reddened and tearstained. She picked him up, hugging him to her body, and immediately he quietened. "Can't you sleep, my sweet precious?" she cooed, as she carried him across the room to check on Sarah. Still sleeping. Amazing considering the racket her brother had made.

The babies might be twins, sharing the same shade of blond hair and similar distributions of baby fat, but they had two distinct personalities. Sean, moody and changeable—like his father—and Sarah unflappable and mild tempered. Was Sarah's disposition characteristic of her mother's?

Jane was removing Sean's damp diaper when she glimpsed Greg standing at the nursery door. He was observing her carefully, his face an unreadable mask. Was that coldness she saw in his eyes? She'd been hopeful earlier, especially when he'd held her hand. Now Jane didn't know what to think. Would she ever be truly welcome, or forever be someone who'd usurped the role that should rightfully be Charlotte's?

Once Jane had finished the diapering, Greg reached for his son. ''I can take over now,'' he said in a voice that brooked no argument. He and Jane made the exchange, Greg noticeably cautious not to touch her, even by so much as a brief brush of his arm. He tucked Sean against his body, and leaned against the doorjamb as his gaze met Jane's head-on, and for the second time, he studied her.

It was then she realized she wasn't wearing her glasses, and her hair—no longer pulled back in a ponytail—was tumbling over her shoulders. The cotton nightshirt she wore wasn't particularly revealing, but it did end well above her knees and showed entirely too much leg and thigh.

She'd been focusing on Charlotte and believing Greg's thoughts to be aimed in the same direction. Instead she saw something entirely different in his gaze. He was looking at her in a way she'd never seen before and for an instant she shivered with excitement at the passion revealed in his dark eyes.

Had Greg changed his mind about wanting her?

There was no mistaking his desire, and she reveled in it. But desire wasn't enough—she couldn't allow hormones to overrule common sense. Hastily she said, "We'd better get some sleep," and scurried to her room.

Get some sleep? Easier said than done, Greg thought as he punched down his pillow in frustration. The attraction had been building all week and it'd taken all his self-control to keep her at arm's length. But this was wrong, all wrong. He couldn't give Jane what she wanted, what she deserved. Jane was looking for love, not just from Sean and Sarah, but from him. And falling in love with her—or anybody—was the last thing in the world he would allow himself to do.

CHAPTER FIVE

GREG heard Jane's shower running the next morning. She was usually up early, but today he'd been the one rising with the twins. He'd spent the last hour thinking about how damnably appealing she'd looked last night, then hating himself for his thoughts.

He'd invited Jane out for a week, but after five days, physical tension was taking its toll, his powers of concentration about shot. He had to make her leave before he did something even dumber than asking her here in the first place.

As soon as the babies were finished with their oatmeal and bananas, Greg put them in the playpen and poured himself another cup of coffee. Hunched over the kitchen table, he was sipping from his mug and working on a strategy when Jane finally came down.

"I've been thinking," Greg began, rising and pouring a cup of coffee for her. Rather than sitting, he gripped the back of the kitchen chair.

"And...?" Jane said.

"It's clear to me that there's no way you'd be contented for long out here."

"I've been thinking, too," Jane said testily, irked that he kept bringing up that wearisome issue. Last night she'd been encouraged that Greg might finally be breaking free of his resistance. But no, here he was again as unyielding as ever and once more trying to tell her how she'd feel. "You couldn't have the slightest inkling of how contented I'd be.

"For some reason you assume that I require constant stimulation, amusement, what have you. Well you're wrong. Been there, done that, as they say. My marriage to Kevin was crammed with activity. Both of us putting in ten- twelve-hour days, hitting the popular night spots in the evening, always on the go. He loved it—I never did. Don't assume I'd ever go back to that sort of existence."

"Is that what caused your divorce?"

"Partially. There were other problems, though…maybe I'll tell you about them sometime. But rest assured, I'm not eager to duplicate that run on the fast track—just the opposite. I've given it a ton of thought and I'm positive I've finally found just what I've been needing for the last couple of years…serenity."

Greg gave her a rueful smile. "Some might say the Circle G is closer to monotony than serenity."

"Not me. When I look around I see the ranch as a safe harbor, a place to drop anchor. I'm thirty-three…at a stage where a change, a settling down, is in order. Remember how the Bible says, 'To every thing there is a season. A time to live and—'"

"A time to die."

Jane momentarily averted her eyes then looked at him somberly. "I didn't mean to bring up sad memories. But this could be *our* season, *our* time for renewal. And I'm confident the path I need to take isn't back in Dallas."

"And you think it's here...with me?"

"And the twins."

"I just don't know." Greg sat, rubbing his chin in thought. Jane could make it seem so logical, so doable.

A knock sounded on the back door and Greg turned in that direction, relieved at the prospect of escape.

"Morning, you two," Elton said, walking in. "Greg, can you drive out to the west pasture with me before we meet the guys? The pond's drying up and we need to cart water to the cattle."

"Sure thing." Greg rose and grabbed his hat off a wall peg. "We'll talk later," he said to Jane on his way out the door.

How can she be that certain? Greg draped his forearms over the steering wheel of a ranch pickup, waiting for Elton to open a gate. They were at the far north end of the Circle G, preparing to spend the day culling out steers for market. But Greg's thoughts weren't on cattle.

This morning, he'd been primed once more to make Jane see reason and once more she'd thwarted him. At first he'd been aggravated that she persisted in delaying the inevitable. But she was so adamant that an arrangement between them was feasible, that he was starting to be persuaded. Could she be right? He hadn't found anyone else, that's for sure. Perhaps he should reevaluate his position. If they established some ground rules, if he could make Jane understand how a marriage between them would be.

"Where's your mind today?" Elton said, reaching in the truck window and snapping his fingers in front of Greg's face. "Or is that a silly question? I can see Jane's got you betwixt and between."

Greg felt compelled to argue. "Then you'd better have your eyes checked."

True to form, Elton paid the comment no mind. "You're worried over what Charlotte would think about all this, aren't you? Well, I was around that little gal all her life and I know sure as I'm standing here that she'd be happy if you found love again."

Greg slapped a hand against the steering wheel. "Now we've gone from 'betwixt and between' to love."

"You trying to tell me you don't have feelings for Jane or her for you? Heck, a blind man could see there's something afoot." Elton took a package of nicotine gum from his pocket and removed a piece.

"I can't speak for her, but my feelings for Jane Jarrett have nothing to do with love." Hearing Elton's grunt of disbelief, Greg added pointedly, "Lust maybe, but not love."

"Lust, hmm?" Elton smirked. "Well, that's as good a place to start as any." He shoved the gum into his mouth and began chewing.

"You never give up, do you?" Greg grumbled. "Quit playing matchmaker and get your rear back in the truck. Here come Wiley and his crew behind us." He gunned the pickup and drove through the gate.

The hot, sweaty work occupied Greg's hands and body that afternoon, but his thoughts were focused elsewhere—on two women. One gone—but leaving him with a promise hanging over his head like Damocles' sword. The other, right here on the ranch, ready and willing to make that promise a reality.

He tried to sift logically through the pros and cons of marrying Jane. No matter how he approached it, there were more pros than cons. Jane would make a wonderful mother. In a matter of days, Sean and Sarah had virtually accepted her as such. They would miss her if she left. He'd miss her, too. Jane had brought a sparkle to their lives. A serenity, too. *Funny, that's the same word she used.*

But how could he allow her to stay, and protect himself in the process? That was the big question. Hour by hour his defenses against her grew weaker. Greg didn't *want* to fall in love. Could he marry Jane, be a decent husband and still armor-plate his heart against that emotion?

Unfortunately, any way he looked at his situation, the bottom line remained the same. He needed a wife. Maybe it would be smarter to search elsewhere, find a woman who wouldn't keep his mind preoccupied with fantasies. But would he be satisfied with any other woman now that he'd met Jane? Greg doubted it. So why was he resisting? He didn't have any good answers.

"May I see you?"

It was late evening that same day and Jane had just put the children to bed when Greg beckoned to her in the downstairs hallway. She followed him into a small office near the rear of the house. It was a man's room, comfortable, utilitarian, free of frills, an overstuffed easy chair and ottoman occupying one corner and a huge antique rolltop desk and swivel chair in the other.

Greg motioned her to sit in the easy chair, then took his place in his desk chair, his back to the desk. She sat quietly, waiting for him to open the conversation.

Greg cleared his throat. "I've told you before I don't *want* a wife," he began.

"Oh, yes, ad infinitum." Jane studied her hands while gauging her next words, then spoke. "I have to confess, though, that I tried to ignore you or pretend that you didn't really know *what* you wanted." She hesitated a moment. "After you came to Dallas, I was delusional enough to believe that given enough time, I would bring you around, change your mind. From the grim expression on your face, I gather I've waged a losing battle."

Rising to her feet, Jane felt decidedly unsteady. She'd thought she hurt before; now the disappointment ran twice as deep. In a strained voice she said, "Don't worry, I won't push myself on you any longer. Give me thirty minutes and I'll be out of—"

Greg rose, too, and stopped her in midsentence, his hands grasping her forearms. "Darn it, hear me out first before you go racing off." Suddenly realizing how close he held her, their faces almost touching, he stood mesmerized, looking down into her eyes, eyes the blue of a morning sky, irresistible eyes. The glasses she'd worn when they first met had soon been abandoned in favor of contact lenses, less temptation for the twins—ten times the temptation for him. Without the barrier of those glasses, her eyes pulled him in like an eddy. Greg could feel himself drowning in that vortex. He leaned closer, then, with a shudder, forced himself to step back.

He'd agonized over this all day and finally come up with a proposition. That was the purpose of this meeting—to try to explain himself to her. Not to enfold her in his arms and kiss her senseless, as he'd almost done. "Uh, why don't you sit back down and listen to what I have to say...please?"

Jane, even more unsteady than before, did as asked. Greg sat also.

"In the short time you've been in my home, I've come to believe you're exactly the mother figure I'd hoped to find for Sean and Sarah. The bond between you three is undeniable. If they had votes in the matter, you'd win them, no contest. But what we're talking about involves more than the twins, it's an irrevocable pact between us—you and me. Can you handle that?"

"I wouldn't want it any other way," Jane said. "I've seen what divorce can do to children. I don't just want to be a mother to them today, next week. I want to be there rooting in the stands at Little League games, listening to their teenage dreams, hearing their—"

"You're missing my point. I mean can you handle a marriage designed to cater to two children's needs instead of your own?" Greg tilted toward her. "I want to be honest with you, but I don't know that what I'm offering is enough."

"I guess the thing to do then is spell out exactly what you're offering and let *me* decide."

"I'm not in love with you." There. The words were out. Not soft-pedaled as he'd intended, but blurted out with all the subtlety of a fist to the stomach. Still, he had to make Jane accept the fact that love couldn't be part of the equation. This was the solution he'd hit upon today, the only way to guard against potential disaster. He'd loved and lost once and was determined to do everything necessary to prevent its happening again.

"Marrying me would be more like a contractual agreement than anything else," he said, trying to ignore her wounded look and its effect on him. "It certainly won't be the kind of match Elton and Nita have. Could you possibly reconcile yourself to that?"

Jane nodded, a lump in her throat. *Reconcile? Maybe. Like? Never.* In the past few days, she realized that her feelings for Greg Merrifield were getting stronger. By marrying him in the face of his disclaimer about love, she would be agreeing to much less than her heart's desire. "What about you?" she asked. "Can you reconcile *yourself* to having another woman in your home? A woman you don't love?"

Greg blanched. The words ricocheting back at him sounded even colder, more repugnant. He avoided a direct answer. "I doubt that either one of us was expecting love in the usual sense, considering the ad and all. That doesn't mean there won't be friendship and caring."

Friendship and caring. Well that was a start, she

thought, and it would be a fuller existence than the one she'd had with Kevin who'd grown selfish and self-absorbed. Yet Jane hesitated. Although romance had never been promised, or even demanded, she felt bereft that the possibility was gone.

"So do you still think it could work, considering what I've told you?" Greg was watching her intently, wanting her to hurry up and respond. Now that he'd made up his mind, there was no point in dragging this out. He might get cold feet again—or Jane might.

"Perhaps this is something I should sleep on."

"I thought you already knew your mind. All week you've been harping on this...why can't you answer me now?"

"Such haste all of a sudden." Then it dawned on her. "It's because of Helga, isn't it?"

Greg paused. "I knew you'd think her leaving triggered everything, but that's not true. Nita's available and I'm sure I could find any number of people in Martinsville who'd lend a hand. But I don't want Sean and Sarah to have a revolving door of nanny-types. I want them to have permanence, preferably to have you."

Jane's head was spinning. She was being offered what she'd been lobbying for—almost—and without another skirmish. Just when she'd conceded defeat, thinking Greg ready to toss her off the Circle G, without warning he'd launched into a discussion of marriage—their marriage.

"Well," she sighed, "it does seem as though

everyone's needs would be served here. Mine, yours...ours.''

"Ours?" One of his eyebrows raised. "Meaning?"

"The babies. My longing to be a mother, yours to find a mother."

He looked at her askance. "And those are our *only* needs?"

Jane felt a hot blush moving up from her neck to her cheeks. "Well, er, uh, after we get to know each other a little better," she stammered, "I'm, uh, willing to give any, ah, wifely obligations a try, too." After all, she was a normal woman and Greg certainly appeared to be a normal man, so it seemed probable that one of these days, they would...would have a somewhat normal marriage.

"'Wifely obligations'?" Greg snorted. "How flattering." He waved his hand with an exaggerated flourish. "Fear not, dear lady, I won't force such *obligations* on you. If you want to be in my bed, it'll be of your own free will—not because of any duty."

Jaws clenched, Greg transferred his gaze from her to the window, staring out at the moonlight, which bathed the rough terrain of his ranch lands in a gentle glow. The view failed to pacify him. He felt like throttling the woman.

All afternoon he'd been telling himself that the one way to guard against getting in over his head was to treat this marriage stuff like a business proposition. But Jane's comment that she'd deign to visit his bedroom as a *favor* ticked him off royally.

"Well, excuse me if I offended you," Jane said

with an embarrassed fury, her blush deepening into a shade Carvel Cosmetics would package as Hot Pink. She took a deep breath. "Obviously what you've so gallantly described to me is the age-old 'marriage of convenience.' That calls for separate bedrooms, don't you think?"

"If that's what you want." Greg was getting madder by the minute. Belligerently he added, "Naturally if you change your mind, I'll be willing to overlook this stipulation and allow you to share mine."

"'Allow' me? Why you egotistical…!" She stood up and slammed a palm on his desk. "What makes you think your bedroom holds any interest for me? Knowing what I know now, I'd sooner hang like a bat from the barn rafters as sleep with you." That said, Jane stormed toward the door, her brain threatening to explode with roiling anger.

Hand on the knob, she wheeled around. "You've done nothing but berate and belittle me from that first telephone conversation, acting like I was some nut case so frantic for a husband, I'd go to any lengths to get one. Well, you're so far off base, it's pathetic."

Jane couldn't remember ever being so put out with anyone. How dare he! And now…now, after so uncharmingly indicating he could take her or leave her, Greg was leaning back in his desk chair, looking dumbfounded and what?—Jane could swear he was trying to stifle a laugh.

"Laugh at me and I'll come over there and flip you right out of that chair. It's not funny. I've put up with you, tried to excuse your behavior, tried to understand that you're resentful over the bad turn your life has taken..." As much as she detested sniffling, sniveling women, once more Jane found herself on the verge of tears. She hastily swiped at her eyes.

Those tears almost drew Greg to her, almost caused him to wrap her in his arms and soothe away her anguish. But he was still smarting over her pronouncement that a sexual relationship with him would be on a par with driving the kids to the dentist or taking out the garbage. He watched as she stood there forlornly and suddenly felt a burst of optimism. She could protest all she wanted to but Jane's actions didn't match her words. She disliked the idea of separate bedrooms as much as he did. A woman didn't get that mad—didn't cry—unless she wanted a guy. Call him perverse, but right now he felt darned smug over her outburst.

She swiped at her eyes again and Greg knew he couldn't leave things this way. He rose from his chair and walked over to her. "I realize you're not to blame for any bad turns in my life and from here on out I'll do my level best not to act that way." He rested a hand on her shoulder, determined not to get into another fruitless battle. "You love my children, don't you?" The twins were always a safe topic.

Jane gazed at him incredulously. "Haven't you been listening? Of course I do. Why would I be here otherwise?"

"You mean here putting up with a lout like me?"

Jane didn't respond.

"All I've been trying to do—ham-handedly, I'm afraid—is warn you that this wouldn't necessarily be the marriage of your dreams." He stepped back and rested a hip on the corner of his desk.

"I've already figured that part out by myself," she said.

"Well, good. So we're straight about it." He paused a moment. "Now, I want to make you a solemn promise—and you know I'm a man who doesn't take promises lightly. I'll always treat you with deference...with respect. I'll support you financially, work at giving you a good life and making this the kind of home you want. Officially your title may be stepmother to the children, but in reality, you'll be the only mother Sean and Sarah will ever know. And a heck of a good one, I'm sure."

Several seconds passed as he waited for her to comment. Stalling for time, she wandered back to her chair and sank down, not sure what to say.

"Well, how about it?" he prompted. "Will you marry me? Will you be a mother to my children?"

Still somewhat dazed, Jane finally nodded her acquiescence. Not exactly an enthusiastic response, but no less spirited than that lackluster proposition of his. She hoped that nothing developed one day that gave her cause for regret, a thought that made her steel her spine. "That is, *yes*, with certain stipulations."

Greg arched an eyebrow, beginning to question the wisdom of bringing up marriage at all. He'd expected to propose, to lay out his cards about his level of commitment, then have her say yea or nay. He hadn't anticipated an argument or a litany of conditions. "Do we need to call in the lawyers and draw up a prenuptial contract?" he gibed. "Make sure we don't miss anything?"

"Don't be facetious. I'm not asking for anything complicated. However, you must agree I'm entitled to at least *one* demand after your sanctimonious declarations."

"I was just trying to be honest about my feelings, avoid leading you on or spouting empty endearments. That was the extent of it. *You're* the one who mentioned separate bedrooms."

"Have it your way," Jane snapped. "I'll accept a limited marriage," she said, "but you have to swear to me that you won't turn to another woman for...for..."

"Sex?" Greg finished for her. He stood up, clenching and unclenching his fists, then walked over to Jane, bracing his hands on the arms of her chair and leaning toward her. "You have no worries on that score. I told you I'm committed to this marriage. That means I won't be looking around for anyone else. I'm not that sort of guy."

"Bully for you. I only hope you mean it."

Hovering almost nose to nose, he glowered at her. "Believe me, if I ever seek any 'female companionship,' it'll be with my own wife." Turning loose of the chair arms, Greg stalked out.

Jane remained in her chair, stunned by what had taken place. This would surely qualify for the *Guinness Book of Records* as history's "least romantic marriage proposal." So why had she gone along instead of tucking tail and running back to Dallas? *Because you'd be more miserable than ever if you did that.* Problems and all, Jane still saw the rocky road of marriage to Greg Merrifield as her best course of action. Likely she should have her head examined.

Greg stood at the refrigerator and downed a tumbler of ice water. All this talk about bedrooms had merely stoked the fire raging within him. He broke into a sweat every time he thought about having Jane in his arms. She possessed such vitality. This latest exchange had been maddening, but he also felt alive, exhilarated. If he and she could strike these kinds of sparks sparring in his office, he could imagine how they'd be upstairs together in the dark of night.

For the first time, Greg knew with absolute certainty that—love or not—he wanted this marriage. And despite Jane's conditions and protestations, he knew she wanted it as well.

He retraced his steps toward his study and encountered her coming down the hall. As far as he was concerned, the die was cast. Now it was up to Jane. "Well, have we hammered out all the provisos?" he said. "Do we have an agreement?"

"I suppose we do," Jane answered, her vexation still in evidence.

"What kind of wedding do you want," he asked, hoping to smooth things over. "Small and simple, or would you like to invite your family, friends...have something elaborate?"

The question caught her by surprise yet she answered without deliberation. "Small and simple." Then a flash of hindsight hit her. *Ohmygosh, my family!* They had no idea what she was about to do.

Pretty sure she could predict their responses, Jane wasn't eager to reveal her plans. Leveling with them would come later. Another one of those bridges she'd cross when the time came. At the rate she was going, there were going to be more bridges in her life than spanned the Mississippi River.

The next Saturday Jane and Greg were married. It was a beautiful day, at least for Texas in the summer, the temperature dipping into the upper eighties and enough fluffy clouds to neutralize the sun's merciless glare. With Jane's concurrence, Greg had arranged for them to be wed in his church, rather than a civil ceremony at the courthouse or at the ranch.

Nita had taken the babies off to her home, giving Jane the morning to herself to prepare for the wedding. Greg was nowhere in sight, having sent Elton to explain that he'd see her at the church.

If the situation had been different, Jane would have appreciated this quaint observance of ritual—the groom not seeing the bride until her walk down the aisle. However, Jane suspected Greg was off somewhere trying to quell the butterflies in his stomach. She could sympathize since her stomach was fluttering, too.

Almost dressed for the wedding, she jerked her head when Elton called to her through the bedroom door, "Hey, in there. Your official chauffeur has arrived. Don't take long. Your groom is waiting."

"Well, this is it," Jane told her mirror, a tight smile reflecting back. She wore a blush pink silk suit and matching pumps, express-ordered from a designer friend in Dallas along with the little veiled hat perched atop her upswept hair. A radical departure in attire from her first wedding.

Then, it had been a showy floor-length gown with a billowy skirt and a beaded train. A flowing veil had framed her face as she walked down the aisle of a gothic-styled church, preceded by eight bridesmaids, a host of friends and family in attendance. Jane didn't long for such pageantry today, but the absence of family brought on a wave of sadness. She willed the distressing thoughts away. Under the circumstances, the simplicity of a small wedding was best. *If only it were the real thing.*

But it was real, Jane reminded herself. Real in the legal sense anyway. She'd accepted the terms, so the disillusionment she felt made no sense. *Remember you wed for love before, and look how that ended up—a disaster. This time it's a different game plan.*

Chastising herself for wasting her energies with unproductive wishful thinking, she grabbed the bridal bouquet Greg had surprised her with—an arrangement of roses, stephanotis and trailing ivy— and headed for the stairs.

The small white country church had a soft warmth that would have been lost in a grand cathedral. The inside, too, was white and today sunlight filtered through stained-glass windows to create a pattern of multiple rainbows. Organ music played by the minister's wife accompanied Jane as, alone, she slowly made her way down the aisle.

Greg stood waiting for her at the end of that aisle, Elton and Nita to his left, each holding a twin. Greg had never looked so handsome, his tan accentuated by the white dress shirt he wore under a gray summer suit. When he glimpsed Jane, his brown eyes seemed to glimmer and a brief smile crossed his face.

Yet the reaction was so fleeting, Jane wondered whether her eyes were betraying her. Reaching the altar, she gazed at Greg again and saw nothing of what was there before. Any glimmer had been replaced by a stern expression and the tightness of his jaw definitely wouldn't accommodate any smiles. Greg looked less like an enraptured groom and more like a felon being sentenced for a capital offense. Maybe in his mind he *was* being sentenced—to a life with a woman he didn't love. Suddenly Jane felt like darting out the nearest door.

Greg tried to calm his panic. The air conditioning had obviously malfunctioned because the temperature in here must be soaring to a hundred and twenty degrees. He'd be lucky to get through the next ten minutes without beads of perspiration popping out on his forehead. He'd prepared himself for getting married, given himself a half-dozen talking-tos, so why was he so shaky? It wasn't as if he hadn't been through all this before, and that time there'd been a large crowd of townspeople as witnesses.

Jane—she's the reason I'm a wreck. From the start, he'd thought her pretty, beautiful. Right now, however, she was gorgeous enough to bring traffic on a busy street to a standstill just by appearing on the curb. There was an aura of elegance and sophistication about her he hadn't seen before. He'd naturally expected her to get gussied up for the wedding, but hadn't anticipated this, this ethereal goddess standing beside him, this vision in pink.

All his voiced concerns about Jane's lifestyle meshing with his raced through Greg's mind. *Am I fixing to botch up the rest of my days?* And hers? The Reverend Hightower was opening his Bible. Well, too late to back out now. At least, too late to back out with any degree of dignity.

Greg glanced over at the twins. Their tiny smiling faces were reassuring. Sean and Sarah looked adorable dressed in the bright cotton outfits Jane had bought them, Sarah's dress decorated with smocking and a ruffled collar and Sean sporting short pants with a white shirt and a tiny bow tie.

He looked at Jane, seeing that her eyes—soft and tender—were focused on the twins also. Greg felt a resurgence of hope. True, there remained problems to resolve, but surely nothing that couldn't be overcome with time and patience. It was either this or a life without Jane. Greg was tired of questioning why that possibility was so disturbing. He just knew it was.

At Greg's nod, the preacher began the age-old vows: "Gregory, repeat after me…"

As Greg spoke, Jane locked gazes with him, wishing she could interpret his thoughts. Or was it better that she couldn't? When her turn came to speak, Jane's voice was low, but firm. Maybe no love existed on Greg's part, but she loved him enough for— Yes love. Whatever the original basis for their marriage, now it was something entirely

different. For her anyway. Jane truly loved Greg
Merrifield. And maybe someday...

"Greg, you may kiss your bride."

Jane raised her face for a brief peck on the lips.
Instead Greg pulled her close, pressing his body
against hers, his lips against hers. Lips that were
hungry and demanding. Caught off guard, for a moment Jane's mouth was unyielding, then her lips
softened under his and parted.

For long seconds all thoughts of others were
eliminated until the flash of a camera and Elton's
laughter brought reality back. Greg loosened his
grasp and turned to the preacher, barely able to
feign a good-natured grin and wrap his arm around
Jane as a congratulatory handshake was offered.

Jane was grateful for the arm. Still reeling from
his kiss, she might have keeled over in a heap without Greg's support. At the moment, it was difficult
to remember her feelings were one-sided and
that—for Greg—the kiss was only ceremonial, this
marriage simply a means to an end. It felt like so
much more.

The nuptials over, Elton thrust his camera into
the gray-haired pastor's hand as they exited the
church. "If you don't mind, Reverend Hightower,
we need lots of pictures to immortalize this occasion."

Greg patiently endured the photo session, the
second picture the two of them flanked by Elton
and Nita with the twins, then a few with the newlyweds alone, followed by more with the children.
In every shot, Greg flawlessly portrayed the role of
doting husband, even pulling Jane's hand to his lips

for a kiss in one. Was it all show, no substance? She didn't have a clue.

The picture taking over, the wedding party returned to the ranch where Nita quickly set up the dining-room table with a lace cloth, plates, flutes, silverware and paper napkins decorated with wedding bells. Elton wheeled in a tea cart with a two-layer wedding cake and a bottle of champagne in a silver ice bucket, then transferred the cake to the center of the table. With Jane by his side, Greg went through the motions of cake-cutting and toasting, but while his toast was kind, "To Jane, with my thanks," it shed no light on his real sentiments and merely left Jane feeling more insecure.

Once the minister and his wife departed, Elton and Nita followed suit. "I feel so bad we can't take the babies tonight," Nita said.

"Don't be silly," Jane answered. "You can't pass up that big family reunion. It's too important."

"But your wedding night...you two oughta have some time to yourselves."

"Not another word." Greg interrupted. "We've got the rest of our lives to be together. Now get on over to those kinfolks in Wichita Falls and don't give us another thought. You've done plenty already."

While Jane washed and put away the dishes and cutlery, Greg exchanged his suit for jeans and a knit shirt, then announced, "If you'll excuse me, I need to run out. Be back in a couple of hours."

"All right," Jane answered, dismayed that he couldn't seem to wait to get away. What did she think? That all of a sudden Greg would drop to his knees and declare he was insanely in love with her? He'd already made his feelings quite clear, and she'd entered into the compact fully apprised of what she could anticipate. So—like it or not—she was going to have to do her best to accept the bargain and stop moaning over what she'd given up.

Still, she couldn't fend off the spasms of melancholy that kept plaguing her. Weddings in her family had always been joyous events, with an abundance of aunts, uncles and cousins in attendance. Sweet little ceremony notwithstanding, this one only paid lip service to joy.

Changing back into casual clothes, she headed toward the nursery. It was here that she would reclaim her equilibrium. She was glad now that Elton and Nita were unable to take the twins for the night. She needed the children with her. *My children.* So today had not been perfect...big deal. All of the tomorrows without Sean and Sarah would have been even more imperfect. She could exist with a lack of romance, even put up with an apathetic husband. "I have my babies and I don't need anything else." A tear trickled down Jane's cheek. The words weren't convincing.

CHAPTER SIX

FOR the next hour, Jane concentrated on the children, playing baby games of peekaboo and pat-a-cake, watching a Barney video, feeding them an early supper. But the demanding day had Sean and Sarah sleepy-eyed by six and Jane realized that bedtime couldn't be put off to its usual hour. She bathed the children, dressed them in pajamas, put them down, then returned downstairs to wait for Greg.

Where could he be? He'd left saying he'd be back in a couple of hours, but two hours had already passed. Jane felt at loose ends. She needed someone to talk to, someone who would be interested, who'd provide a bit of tender concern that she was temporarily groomless. Yet the ones she'd always counted on—her family—didn't even know about this marriage.

A stab of conscience hit Jane. Supposedly frolicking on vacation, instead she'd sneaked off and gotten married—to a man who was a total stranger to them, and a near stranger to her. Not that Jane felt she'd had a choice as to the telling. There would have been howls of protest and hours of discussion from every quarter. That's why she'd decided not to tell everyone until after the ceremony. However, she couldn't keep putting off the inevitable. Jane dialed her parents' number.

"Janie, this is crazy." Her father's reaction had been exactly as anticipated.

"But we love each other." Jane knew it was the only thing she could say that would reassure him, yet it bothered her to be less than honest. "And the babies are adorable."

"If it's really love," Jim Jarrett said, "then it could have waited. At least until you brought him and the twins home to meet us."

Renee Jarrett was equally critical. "It's not like you to be so rash, sugar."

"If I remember correctly," Jane reminded her, "you and Daddy married less than a month after you met. Why is this any worse?"

"You can't compare our circumstances to yours," Renee scolded. "We were in love, madly, impetuously in love. Are you sure this isn't about Greg Merrifield's children rather than the man himself?"

Having been witness to Jane's distress over her infertility, it wasn't a stretch for Renee to reach that particular conclusion. A few weeks ago she would have been correct. But now things had changed. "As I told Daddy, I'm in love, Mother."

"Oh, sugar, loving two babies and loving a man are two different issues."

Jane could see that arguing was futile. She should have better prepared her parents for this turn of events. With a bit of advance notice, they would have had time to absorb the shock. "Everything will be okay, Mom. Please help me on this. Explain things to the rest of the family and try to make them understand."

Her mother must have caught the desperation in her voice, because she paused, then agreed. "I'll do what I can. We love you, Janie."

"And I love you. I'll call you soon. Bye." Jane hung up the receiver and emitted a loud sigh.

"Regrets already?" Greg was home and standing behind her, touching her shoulders.

Jane wanted to lean back into those strong hands, to have Greg take the remorse away. "No regrets, but a megadose of guilt," she said. "I just told my parents of our marriage. Now I feel dreadful over keeping them in the dark. They'll forgive me, of course," she said, slumping against the doorjamb, "but that doesn't help at the moment."

"Maybe I have just what the doctor ordered." He gestured across the kitchen where hot and cold food containers plus a take-out bag and a bottle of wine sat on the counter. "I asked a restaurant in Amarillo to prepare us a wedding dinner," Greg said.

"You went all the way to Amarillo?"

"Wiley flew me down. Didn't mean to take so long, but I had something special in mind." He grinned. "It's not Dallas cuisine, but I hope you'll be pleased."

Jane was. Here she'd been moping around, thinking her husband was ignoring her when he'd been off on a pleasure mission—her pleasure. "I can't believe you went to all this trouble."

He kissed her forehead. "You're worth a little trouble. After we put Sean and Sarah to bed, we can eat and talk." He glanced around. "Where are they?"

"Already asleep. I guess all the activity today wore them out."

"Let me kiss them good-night, then I'll tend to the feast."

He tiptoed into the nursery and gazed down at his two offspring. Both were sleeping soundly, yet when he touched them, Greg saw smiles appear on their small faces. He could swear there was relief in those smiles. Greg felt a sense of relief as well. It was as if once he and Jane had uttered those "I dos," every last shackle of grief and indecision had been torn off—that hope had returned to his life. Grinning, he walked back downstairs to join his wife.

"No, let me do the serving," he told Jane, who was opening cartons. "You stay out until I call you."

Fifteen minutes later, she was signaled back to a table fully set, with candles and her bridal flowers as a centerpiece.

"You did this all by yourself?"

"With a little advice and assistance from the restaurant manager," he admitted, pouring the wine.

The meal—lamb on skewers and Greek salad—was delicious. First they talked about the food, the children, then relaxed by the wine, the conversation became more personal as they eased into a rehash of the wedding.

"Elton's proud as a peacock that his ad idea worked so well."

"I still have difficulty believing he was the one who thought that up. Sure it wasn't Nita?"

"Nope. Both give him the credit. Especially him.

Practically broke his arm patting himself on the back. He's so full of himself now that he'll probably seek out a part-time slot as advice columnist for the *Martinsville Weekly*.''

"Greek food is a favorite of mine," Jane noted, popping a dark olive into her mouth.

"Me, too," he said.

"I'm surprised a cattleman would own up to that, or even allow lamb on his menu."

Greg placed a finger to his lips. "Promise you won't tell anyone, but I love lamb. Truth is, though, I'll eat almost anything. Even sushi."

"Sushi, hmm? Don't remember seeing a sushi bar in these parts. Amarillo, again?"

"This rancher has occasionally wandered off the range, even further away than Amarillo." Greg laughed, a deep robust laughter.

"Oh, and what exactly were you doing on those jaunts?"

"You'll find out over time. Can't reveal everything at once. We'd be left with nothing to talk about and you'd be bored with me."

I doubt that could happen in a million years. "So that's it? Your penchant for Greek food and sushi is all you plan to reveal tonight? Surely you can risk future boredom and share one or two more tidbits." Jane leaned on the table, her finger tracing the rim of her wineglass.

"Well, maybe one or two. My new favorite color is green." He reached over to finger the collar of Jane's cotton shirt, a soft mint shade. "And I'm growing rather fond of women tall enough to kiss without getting a crick in my neck."

"Women?" she teased.

He winked. "No, definitely not 'women'." It was one particular woman who had him stewing. That kiss at the end of the ceremony was still singeing his lips. If he didn't watch himself, he'd be making moves on Jane before they got to the baklava.

For other bridegrooms, that wouldn't be unusual. But Jane wasn't ready, and he intended to give her as much time as she needed. He cared about her feelings and he had no intention of making her think the meal or any other gesture was merely a device for luring her to his bed.

Greg couldn't really explain it to himself, but he'd wanted to do something extraordinary tonight, something to make up for the lack of a romantic courtship. He'd thought the dinner might be a start.

Not that he didn't plan on getting her in his bed. Greg intended to make Jane his wife in every sense of the word. But he was going to take it slow and easy. He wanted her, but trying to make tonight special wasn't about sex. It was about this marriage, its permanence, its survival.

"Okay, you know my favorite color and my secret appetites." *Some of them anyway.* "Now tell me more about Jane Jarr—Merrifield."

"Like what? Aren't you the one who cut me off one day, saying you didn't want an autobiography?"

"Impossible," he said self-mockingly. "I'd never do such a thing."

She smiled. "Where shall I begin?"

"How about your marriage, Kevin...start with

him,'' Greg said. ''Tell me more about the dolt who was willing to give you up.'' He grinned ruefully. ''The other dolt, that is, not that Merrifield maniac who tried to run you off the Circle G.''

Jane laughed, pleased that Greg really did want to know about her. She pushed her plate away and began discussing her years with Kevin. His jealousy about her job, how he blamed her when she couldn't get pregnant.

''I can't believe that guy, not being able to see how desperate you were for children.''

''I don't think Kevin ever saw past his own needs.''

''Selfish creep,'' Greg said.

''He would say you only have my version of the story. Regardless, the marriage was a mistake, something that should have ended long before it did.''

Greg had been the one who'd brought up the past so Jane decided to follow his lead. There were things about Charlotte still undiscussed, things to get out in the open.

''I don't mean to upset you,'' she began cautiously, ''but I'd like to hear more about Charlotte. If I'm to care for the twins, to be a good mother, I need to know about her. Sean and Sarah are going to ask questions one of these days and I want to be able to give them answers.''

Greg carried their plates to the sink, then refilled their wineglasses and sat back down. He really didn't want to talk about Charlotte, but Jane was right. She'd been candid about her marriage. He owed her as much. They might as well bring out all the ghosts and be done with it.

"We knew each other all our lives," he said. "Our parents were best friends and neighbors, their spreads separated only by one ranch. Charlotte was ten years younger, but we were constantly together. Birthday parties, domino and card games, family dinners, what have you...

"For years, she was like my little sister, then one day a grown-up girl appeared in my view and my feelings became less brotherly. At some point everyone started assuming we'd marry. It sort of became expected."

"And you didn't mind?"

"Oh, no, Charlotte was an easy person to love."

"Still, she must have been young when you married."

"Too young actually—only eighteen and fresh out of high school. In a way I felt like she was being cheated. I'd gone off, finished college, been in the military, traveled some...she hadn't done any of those things. But she was okay with that. Our folks, too. In fact, they supported our decision to marry. Maybe some kind of blind intuition on their part."

"Elton told me they were killed right after you two married."

Greg nodded. "My dad owned a small plane. The four of them were flying to Vegas for the weekend and got caught in a violent thunderstorm over New Mexico. They went down in the mountains. No survivors."

"You and Charlotte were both only children?"

"Right. Suddenly we only had each other—that and two ranches to run. We put off having kids for a few years, too busy working the ranches. Plus an opportunity came up to buy the spread between our two properties. The Ibsens were retiring to town and made us an offer we couldn't refuse. Now we had three ranches."

Greg pushed away from the table and stretched out his long legs. "When we were finally ready to take on a family, there were several miscarriages. The twins were like our last hope."

"Was Charlotte already pregnant with Sean and Sarah when the leukemia was discovered?"

"Yeah. The doctors suggested abortion so she could have the kind of treatment that might save her life. She wouldn't hear of it, adamant that the babies' lives were too important. I guess you can see why Sean and Sarah mean the world to me."

Jane nodded. Greg had suffered a number of heartbreaks. Yet she knew it was a good sign that he'd consented to talk about them. Not only had he wanted to discuss her past, but had been willing to reveal more of his own story as well.

"So what's it like being part of a large family?" he asked, clearly ready for a change in topics.

Jane took the cue. Enough heartrending talk. "Chaotic," she answered dryly. "Wait till you meet them all. Mom, Dad, two brothers, two sisters, their spouses and children. Prepare to be overwhelmed. Everyone lives in Dallas or one of the suburbs so there are family functions galore and usually a new grandbaby to celebrate."

"Was it difficult to be around babies when you couldn't have one of your own?"

Jane was surprised by Greg's insightful question. She nodded. "I'd just learned I was—" she paused, the memory still hurtful "—that I was…unable to get pregnant…when my brother's wife had a baby boy. It was their first child so naturally they were elated. Yet everyone was walking on eggs to protect my feelings and I felt like the two of them were being robbed of a measure of joy because of 'Poor Jane.'"

"You were divorced by then?"

"Yes, my marriage was already finished when I learned for certain I couldn't bear children. Kevin thought all along I was faking the medical complications, accused me of caring too much about—" Jane stopped. She'd almost said career. Things were going too well for her to open that can of worms.

"About?" Greg prompted.

"My figure."

"The clod."

"My brothers had nastier names for him. It was all I could do to prevent them from beating him to a pulp. They consoled themselves instead with fiendish plots of torture. Jeff wanted to hang Kevin up by his thumbs. Craig's fantasy torment was staking Kevin out on a fire-ant hill."

"They sound like my kind of guys."

Jane smiled. "I think you'll like them when you get around to meeting them."

"I do want to meet everyone, Jane, and soon," Greg said, surprising her. "Sean and Sarah should know their cousins, their aunts and uncles and new grandparents. I hadn't really thought about it before, but maybe they need more than just a mom and dad.''

"I appreciate that," she said. She wasn't sure he'd accede so willingly to introductions. But he'd gone her one better in seeing the advantages of an extended family. Once more it was evident how much Greg loved his son and daughter. If only he could spare a tiny portion of love for her.

The meal over, Greg had brewed a pot of coffee and suggested they take their cups to the family room when Jane heard a cry from upstairs. "That sounds like Sarah," she said, starting for the nursery.

The next hours were spent coddling a feverish baby. "Should we call the doctor?" Jane asked, pressing her lips against a tiny hot forehead.

"Not this soon. Let's try to get the fever down first," he said, administering drops of children's Tylenol. "Probably a twenty-four-hour virus."

"You've obviously been through this before."

"In the early months, I panicked and rushed them to the pediatrician with every little cough or sniffle. Now I know what's serious and what's not. Still, if Sarah's not better by morning, we'll have her checked out." Greg went to pick up Sean, who'd been awakened by his sister and was vying for his share of attention.

Caring for the children brought Jane back to earth. Greg might have gone to extra effort to make the evening festive, but a nice meal and a bit of conversation were just that. No more. She had to quit looking for cues that he was falling in love or she'd drive herself crazy. Married or not, they were still in the process of getting acquainted. Too soon to wish for more. Yet Jane felt they'd moved forward by leaps and bounds in the past few hours.

It was almost three a.m. when the children were quiet again. Jane pulled a lightweight cotton blanket over Sarah and caressed the baby's forehead. No trace of fever. She left the nursery, Greg right behind her.

"Well, good night," she said, standing in the hallway. She stood on tiptoes and kissed Greg's cheek, then stepped back.

For what seemed an eternity, he stared down at her, his eyes searing into hers. Jane's pulse accelerated, but she held her feelings in check. The next move was up to Greg.

When he didn't make one, she resignedly said "good night" again and opened the door to her bedroom. *Why doesn't he argue, say this is no place for me, that I should be spending the night with him?* But Greg said nothing.

Jane closed the door behind her and leaned against it, hoping for his knock. A knock that didn't come. After long moments, the band of light from the hallway went out.

"Some wedding night," Greg groaned aloud, pulling off his watch and laying it on the dresser. Sure, this was what he'd agreed to, but he could see that biding his time would not be easy. He'd hoped for Jane to take the initiative, but instead she had bestowed a sisterly peck on the cheek. To him that set the limits for tonight. Tarnation.

Well at least the woman was his now. They were

bound together tighter than a trussed turkey and she couldn't get away. The notion brought a smile to Greg's lips. He'd just give her a while to get used to the idea. In the meantime, he'd get used to cold showers.

"Sleep well?" Greg asked as Jane walked into the kitchen the next morning, carrying the twins. He got up from the table, helped her place them in high chairs, served them apple juice, then sat back down and resumed reading the newspaper, passing a couple of sections her way.

"You mean the four hours after we went to bed?" Jane poured her own coffee, then sat down across from Greg, chin propped on her hands, paper ignored. Unless World War III had broken out overnight, there'd be few news items that could hold her attention today.

She'd barely slept a wink and it was all Greg's fault. Those thoughtful gestures, those smoldering glances. She wanted him. Yet here he was, Sports section in hand, totally absorbed. It was vexing that he was acting like they'd been married ten years, instead of one day.

Greg peeked at Jane over his newspaper. He was trying to keep things even, to pretend that this was a regular family morning at the breakfast table, but at the moment he was all caught up in his wife's sleepy lusciousness. He couldn't remember one blasted word about preseason football.

"Obviously *you* slept well," she said, noticing he was watching her.

"Perfectly," he lied. "Even though a wedding

night alone takes some getting used to," he muttered behind his paper.

"What?"

"Nothing."

"If you have something to say, say it."

"I was merely thinking out loud about our *sleeping* arrangements."

"What's wrong with them?"

"Nothing. My room's at one end of the hall and yours is at the other. Who could improve upon that?" he asked caustically.

"Are you trying to provoke me?"

"Course not. It's not like we're on our *honeymoon* or anything. If we were, I'd have said something about the abundance of moon last night and the lack of 'honey.'"

"Well, thanks for refraining from saying it."

"You're welcome. However, I can't guarantee that it might not come up again once or twice in the next fifty years."

Fifty years. That could be a lot of squabbling if they kept on like this. "Listen, why don't we just start today over," she said.

"Fine with me...so good morning. Shall we have some breakfast?"

"Let's. Since you served supper, I'll do the honors."

No sooner had they begun eating than the telephone rang. Greg answered, then passed the receiver to Jane. "It's for you."

"And everyone always thought you were the cautious sister and I the frivolous one," tittered the voice on the line. It was Catherine, her younger sister. "Was that delicious-sounding guy just now the new bridegroom?"

"Yes," Jane answered.

"I should have welcomed him to the family while I had him on the line. I can't wait to see if the face and bod match the voice. Do they?"

"I'm sure you'd think so." *My sister,* Jane mouthed to Greg, grateful that he could hear only one side of this conversation.

He nodded and resumed eating his breakfast.

"We both know I'm a sucker for good-looking men," Catherine agreed with a giggle. "Just think, you meet the guy a month ago on that job in Amarillo and bam, you're in love. Romantic."

So that's the story Renee had fed the family. *Thank you, Mother.* "And how's, uh, everyone doing?"

"So you're not going to offer any comment on what I just said. Is hubby sitting there, taking in your conversation?"

"You might say that. Have you talked to Mom and Dad?"

"Oh my, yes. Daddy's wringing his hands and Mom's telling everyone it's high time you found a little happiness. You *are* happy, aren't you, Jane?"

"Of course I am. Sean and Sarah are wonderful."

"Is Greg Merrifield wonderful, too?"

"As you well know, he's close by, monitoring my every word. Do you want the guy's ego inflating like the Goodyear Blimp?"

"How could his ego be anything but inflated after snagging you?" Catherine said. "I'm glad you're happy, Jane. Come home soon. And bring your new family with you.''

Jane returned the portable phone to its cradle on the kitchen wall, then carried her plate to the sink, scraping the now-cold breakfast into the garbage disposal. Her appetite had vanished. If only she *were* as happy as she'd pretended to her sister.

"What's going to cause my ego to inflate?"

"Just sister talk."

"Secrets from your husband? Tsk, tsk."

"Everyone has secrets," Jane hedged.

"Not too many I hope. After all—" The telephone ringing again stopped Greg in midsentence. He answered and again it was for Jane. "I suppose it's one of your brothers this time."

It wasn't a brother, but her agent, Ron Gold. "What's this ridiculous thing you've gone and done?" he said without preamble.

"And so nice to hear from you, too," Jane snapped back, evading the question and wishing she could carry the phone into another room. But that was impossible. Greg had already kidded her about secrets. If she acted as if she were hiding something, he wouldn't be quite as amused.

"I hear you got married yesterday—and to a guy you just met. Saints alive, Jane! I don't know whether I should be mad as blue blazes that you're playing havoc with your career or simply worried sick that you've lost your mind."

Jane counted to ten. Ron ought to be horsewhipped for calling up the day after her wedding and carrying on like this. But that was Ron. Business took precedence over everything in his mind.

He did care about her, though, and they enjoyed a good working association, even if occasionally Jane thought her agent saw dollar signs each time he looked at her.

"You know you won't be happy out there in 'Bubbaville,'" Ron growled. "I want you to forget this trumped-up marriage and come home to Dallas. Pay attention to your modeling. Carvel may have done you dirty, but something better's going to come your way. Any day now."

This conversation had gone on too long. Entirely too long. Greg was glaring at her as if she and Ron were negotiating the sale of classified data. "I've got to go," Jane said.

"Well, if you think I'm going to give up without a fight," he exclaimed, "you don't know me very well."

"I know you all too well. But you're wasting your time."

Ron harrumphed. "I'll be the judge of that. I'll be back in touch."

As soon as she was off the phone, Greg started in on her. "Not a brother at all, hmm, but a discarded boyfriend."

"No, not a boyfriend. Ron's my—" *Should I say agent? Is this my opening to tell Greg about my career?* Jane hesitated, then decided to wait until their relationship settled a bit more. There was still plenty of time for sharing. "Ron's just a pal," she said.

"Pal, huh? Well, if he calls again, *I'll* be the one telling him he's wasting his time." With that threat hanging, he left the room, taking the children with him.

Too bad he couldn't have done so a few minutes earlier. Jane would have used the opportunity to convince Ron that her modeling days were over. That she'd started a new life and was committed to it. Even if her new husband was behaving like a jealous suitor at the moment. *Jealous?* Jane smiled. Now, that notion was altogether pleasing.

The telephone rang a third time just as Greg reentered the kitchen. "You might as well answer," he said. Still, he didn't leave the kitchen, merely began clearing his dishes from the table, and staying close enough to hear Jane's side of any conversation.

"Just wanted to say 'Congratulations.'" It was her other sister, Melissa, the only person Jane had told about the ad.

"Thank you," Jane answered warily.

"And how's the honeymoon going?" Melissa asked enthusiastically. "Nonstop passion?"

"That comment doesn't deserve an answer." Jane feigned a soft laugh, a laugh she hoped would be persuasive.

"Guess not." Melissa laughed also. "But tell me—*does* he look like Roy Rogers?"

"Mel…"

"Oh, there's a warning in that tone. Like don't tell Mom and Dad, hmm? No worry. I'll never spill the beans. But my silence has its price."

"Name it." *There goes that black beaded dress Melissa's had her eye on.* Well, that was fine, Jane thought. She had little use now for all those high-stepping outfits that were jamming the condo's closets.

But Melissa wasn't referring to clothes. "Be happy with your cowboy, okay?"

"I'll do my best," Jane said, sheepish for thinking the worst of her sister.

"And in the meanwhile, give that lucky groom a kiss for me, will you?"

"Sure, thanks. And Mel?"

"Yes?"

"Next time we see each other, that black dress you like is yours."

With an "ooh!" sounding in her ear, Jane hung up the phone. She thought of the irony in Melissa's request. Kissing the groom. Very funny. The only real kiss they'd shared was that one at the end of the wedding ceremony. And all it had accomplished was to leave her yearning for another, and another. But from all indications, there wouldn't be a repeat performance anytime soon. Unless she initiated it. *Now what imp put that notion in my mind?*

The more Jane thought about the idea, the more appealing it became. It would do Greg good to have his nose tweaked a bit. She walked over to the sink and tapped him on the shoulder.

When Greg turned, Jane pressed her lips against his briefly. "From my sister," she said, backing away. "I was instructed to give the groom a smooch for her."

Greg's hands on her waist spun Jane around and now she was trapped between him and the counter. "Surely she expected you to do better than that." Suddenly his lips were on hers and this kiss was even more high-octane than the one at the wedding. With his mouth and his body pressed tightly against hers, Jane could feel her knees turn rubbery. His lips coaxed hers to part so he could more fully claim what she'd impulsively offered. The kiss seemed endless, yet ended all too soon as Greg released her and stared down into her face, his arms still around her.

"Why don't we get out for a while?" he said, smiling. "Take the twins for a ride."

An outing was the farthest thing from her thoughts. Suddenly self-conscious and concerned that he could see straight to her fast-beating heart, Jane pushed away and tightened the sashes of her robe. She hadn't expected the intensity of that kiss—even though she had started it. She hadn't expected that smile, either, or her pent-up desire to smile back—to smile the way a woman does at the man she loves.

They spent the day touring the ranch, she and Greg in the front seat of his minivan, Sean and Sarah in car seats in the back. Jane had known the ranch was large, but she was unprepared for the vastness: acre upon acre of sun-scorched land, dotted with cattle, a few fields that had grown wheat, now plowed under in preparation for a fall planting.

At noon they stopped for lunch at a barbecue restaurant. Judging by the vehicles parked outside, the crowd was an equal mix of ranchers and truckers.

The waitress Jackie, a friendly type in cowgirl

fringe, heaps of hair and layers of eye makeup, took to the twins at once.

"Aren't you just the darlingest things I've ever seen!" she squealed, giving each chubby cheek a squeeze. "Jackie'll just have to take you home with her."

Sarah responded with a grin and a slap on the plastic high chair tray. Sean picked up on the sound and both began a vigorous pounding. The restaurant was noisy, but the children were even noisier and heads were turning. Hastily Greg unwrapped a package of crackers to keep their tiny hands busy and quiet.

As Jane and Greg ate their way through platters of brisket, red beans and coleslaw, the twins worked their way through bananas and milk, some of the beans and multiple packages of crackers. Both their faces were now coated with various portions of the meals and the high chair trays looked like a food collage.

"Wonder if Jackie will still want to take them home after she sees this mess," Greg said.

"She'll probably make us swear an oath never to come back during her shift," Jane answered.

But Jackie, clean washcloths in hand, was totally unperturbed by the squalor before her. "Let me wipe those cute little faces for you." She turned to Jane. "Honey, you are one lucky lady—these precious twins and a husband other women would kill for." She ripped off the check from her pad and laid it on the table.

Greg chuckled as the waitress left their table. "Jackie gets a big tip for her perceptiveness." He reached for the check. "Come on, lucky lady, time for more sight-seeing."

Jane smiled to herself. Today was the sort of day she had fantasized about. She thought of the raw truth in Jackie's candid statement. The waitress was right. Jane had almost everything a woman could wish for.

She tried not to focus too heavily on the "almost" part. If she went back to Dallas, the old troubles would be lying in wait for her. She'd still be infertile, still be unemployed, still aimless—and she'd definitely be unhappy. No, marrying Greg had to be a better alternative than her old life. She was simply going to have to apply all her energies to working things out.

That evening they shared a light meal of soup and salad. After dinner, she and Greg played with the twins in the den.

Sean had mastered walking before Jane's initial arrival at the Circle G, but tonight he was apparently in training for a future climb of Mount Everest. Dragging along a love-battered teddy bear as he explored, he crawled onto the coffee table, then scaled the back of the sofa. Three times he had to be pulled back.

The floor wasn't much safer because of his fascination with wall plugs and telephone cords. Both Jane and Greg were kept busy rescuing him from dangerous territory. "This is exhausting," Greg said, "but I hate to keep him confined to that kiddie corral every single minute." He gestured toward the playpen.

Sarah was sitting in a child-size rocking chair,

quietly turning the pages of a cloth-covered book. "Do you want to read a story, too?" Jane said to Sean, picking up the little boy and hoping to divert his attention.

"Ma Ma," Sean said with a smile and Jane was torn between being elated and worried about Greg's reaction. "Ma Ma," the baby repeated.

"He's finally beginning to talk like his sister." Greg lifted the baby from Jane's arms. "Now say Da Da. Okay, Sean? Da Da."

Jane held her breath, hoping Sean would cooperate.

"Da," he said, patting Greg's cheek.

"That's my boy. Now go to Jane, er, your mama."

Jane sat on the sofa holding her son, a sappy grin on her face. Today had been close to perfect. Only one element was missing—Greg's love. But she would not mar the moment by asking for more miracles when she had so many already.

CHAPTER SEVEN

DURING the week following the wedding Greg left ranch labors to others and concentrated on his new family. There were more morning outings with the twins, lunch at various local spots, returning to the ranch in time for the children's naps.

Afternoons were spent relaxing—watching rented movies on television, reading and talking. It was during those lazy hours together that the bond between Jane and Greg strengthened.

On Wednesday, he explained the need to spend a few hours in his office, tending to paperwork. "This is the part of ranching I hate," he said when Jane popped in to bring him fresh-squeezed lemonade.

"Can I help?"

"I'm almost finished. Just trying to catch up on a mound of stuff I've been putting off too long. Seems that with the babies and the ranch I'm always busy. It's easier to procrastinate about those jobs you can close off in a room." Greg hadn't realized until he sat down to pay the bills just how much he had procrastinated.

The most crucial item pending was the probate of Charlotte's will. A distasteful, but necessary task, which hadn't seemed all that pressing. Other tasks were more urgent—attending to the babies' needs, the ad business and now marrying Jane. But he shouldn't have neglected the probate so long. It was becoming a financial imperative to have it completed. He'd make an appointment with his lawyer for next week.

"Well, I won't interrupt any longer," Jane said. She was still lingering at the door. "I'll be glad to assume some of the paperwork burden, though. All you have to do is say the word."

He wagged a finger at her. "Better be careful. I might just take you up on that."

"I wish you would. I'd like to do something. My ranching knowledge may not extend past recognizing one end of a cow from the other, and as far as farming...well I can't even grow houseplants. But I'm pretty good on the computer so maybe some correspondence?"

"You have your hands full as it is. The children, meals..." Greg didn't want Jane to think he was taking advantage of her by asking for too much.

"Not really," she said, sitting down across from him. "Since Nita's niece was hired to do the cleaning and laundry, I'll have more time." If their marriage was to develop the way Jane wanted it to, she was going to have to share in more than just the children.

He looked at her steadily, then handed over a ledger sheet. "You could double-check this column of figures. Here's a calculator."

Thus Jane began taking a part in running the ranch.

On Thursday he suggested driving into town. I'll introduce you to Martinsville's version of a supermarket." That was another thing that was changing about their relationship—Greg's willingness to indoctrinate her into his world.

After supper that evening, she made chocolate chip cookies, one of her specialties. "Those fattening chocolate chip cookies again?" he bantered playfully, patting his stomach. "Keep this up and I'll have to add a weight room onto the barn."

"As I recall, *you* were the one who pitched three bags of chocolate chips into our shopping cart. But if you don't feel right eating the cookies, I'm sure Elton and the guys will be willing to take them off my hands tomorrow."

"Oh, no you don't." Greg snatched a hot cookie and juggled it in his hands. "We're not wasting homemade goodies on those characters."

Jane could sense Greg was becoming more comfortable with the marriage. So was she. She liked the laid-back atmosphere at the ranch, being able to be her own person and to wear what she chose rather than subjected to the dictates of the camera or public appearances. She liked the camaraderie of Elton and assorted ranch crew dropping by for a quick glass of tea or a Coke, appreciated their care not to intrude on the "honeymooners." In their own way they were extending hands of welcome, making a place for her.

Her life was operating at a much slower pace, yet there was no trace of tedium. Greg's early predictions about her pining away for city amenities had borne no fruit. Learning about the ranch, looking after the babies and being with Greg filled the daylight hours to capacity. Each moment brought a new joy, a deeper contentment, and so many wonderful discoveries, especially about Sean and Sarah.

"Did you see that?" she said on Saturday evening, grabbing Greg's arm to get his attention. They were in the family room on the couch, watching the children playing on the rug. Sean was stacking blocks, placing a third one precariously atop two other teetering ones. "He's really coordinated. And look at that little face, that forehead all scrunched up with concentration." The blocks tumbled over and for a moment Jane thought the boy was going to cry. Instead he started rebuilding his stack. "That's it, sweetie, don't give up."

"The Merrifield men are determined," Greg said, resting his booted foot across his knee. Sarah toddled up to him and raised her hands to be picked up. "So are the Merrifield women. Come up here, pretty girl." Greg lifted Sarah and kissed her nape, evoking a giggle. "Luf Da," she said, patting Greg's face.

"That's right, precious. 'Da' loves you, too. Now go to your mama. Da's going to help Sean stack blocks." Greg got up from the couch and sat cross-legged on the floor with his son.

Jane watched her new family reflectively, knowing that the four of them presented a picture of bliss, precisely the family image she'd longed for. Today marked their one-week anniversary. In that time Greg seemed to have accepted her as the twins' mother, referring to her as "Mama" easily. And she never failed to react with inward pleasure when she heard the word.

Occasionally she wondered if she'd ever fill a

more meaningful role than mother to Sean and Sarah and companion to him. Greg had certainly demonstrated no inclination for her to be anything else. He'd sit beside her, even touch her now and then—a tap, a pat—but the touches were more buddy-like than romantic. Jane was surprised he hadn't popped her on the arm with his fist in that age-old bonding ritual of guys.

As often as Jane told herself she should be satisfied with the status quo, with the bargain made, in the deep dark of night she couldn't keep from thinking about the love that was missing.

What about those kisses? she asked herself. The one at the wedding could be chalked up to show-boating—Greg's trying to live up to the expectations of Elton, Nita and the Reverend and Mrs. Hightower. But what about that second one in the kitchen? There'd been no audience then.

Yet as much as Jane would prefer believing passion had triggered the kiss that teased her memory, she knew retaliation had been the likely impetus. Her sister's suggestion had set the wheels in motion and she'd followed through with that impulsive peck on the cheek. Greg had merely finished what she'd started. His kiss might have been explosive, but it carried no greater significance than the fact of calling her bluff.

"I'm proud of you, boy," Elton said. It was mid-morning on the following Monday and Greg was back at work. The two of them were loading cattle feed into the bed of Elton's pickup, the supplemental food necessitated by the year's low rainfall.

"How's that?" Greg hefted a bag of grain onto the tailgate, then pulled out a handkerchief to mop his brow.

"Well, I wasn't sure how you'd take to this marriage thing. Afraid it happened because I was pushing so hard, bringing up your promise to Charlotte so often." Elton poured a cup of water from a cooler in the truck's cab. "But you've put my worries to rest. Looks like you just might forgive me for keeping the pressure on," Elton said with a grin.

"And it looks to me like you're taking bows again." Greg cocked an eyebrow.

"Guess I am. Just wanted to tell you that I'm proud of how seriously you're taking this marriage, and the way you're courting your wife."

Leave it to Elton to blow everything way out of proportion. "I *am* serious about making the marriage work, but your crazy assumption that I'm 'courting' is farfetched even for you."

"That lovesick expression on your face says something else. Why whenever your bride's around, you're beginning to look downright—"

"I thought Cupid wore a diaper and carried a bow and arrow," Greg grumbled, his face reddening. "You'll soon have me picking wildflowers and bringing home boxes of candy."

"Wouldn't be a bad idea. Women like that sort of thing." Elton draped an arm around Greg's shoulder. "It's been over a year, boy," he reminded Greg affectionately. "Like I've told you before, nothing wrong with getting on with your life, with loving again."

There was no arguing with Elton when he got in

one of these moods. Greg plopped his hat back on his head and picked up another bag of grain. Maybe work would distract his foreman.

However, work didn't divert Greg's attention from the conversation. Did he have a hangdog look when Jane was around? He recognized his growing fondness for her, but that was fortuitous considering she was his wife. And yes, he was attracted to her—any red-blooded American male would be.

But it was more than Jane's beauty that drew him. She was giving and undemanding… Greg's lips curved in a smile. Never in a million years would he have expected to be referring to that woman who'd cajoled and wheedled her way into his life as undemanding. How things had changed. Perhaps he should just throw caution to the wind and enjoy what he had. Maybe he should allow himself to love Jane. Maybe he already did.

Jane was in the kitchen alone when Greg arrived home that afternoon. He was dirtier than she'd ever seen him, mud-streaked jeans and shirt matched by a grimy face, shadowed with beard. His boots and hat had apparently been left on the porch. "Elton and I were mending cross fences when the rain started," he explained. "Smack in the middle of a pasture when the storm blew in and the truck got stuck. Had to dig it out. Am I a mess or what?" he laughed.

Jane felt encouraged that Greg was in a good mood. All day she'd been sweating over her plans, wondering how Greg would take them.

"Well, at least the rain was needed, even if you did get stuck," she said.

"Yes. Elton thought it was hilarious. Of course, he was the one driving the truck and I was the one in the mud pushing." Greg stood there for a moment watching Jane, as if searching for something else to say, but all he managed was, "I'd better go on and get cleaned up."

He came back downstairs thirty minutes later, joining Jane and the children in the family room. She'd fetched him a cold beer from the refrigerator and had it waiting on the coffee table. "Oh, the pleasures of a devoted wife," he said, taking a drink.

The pleasant atmosphere gave Jane courage to broach the topic that had been troubling her most of the afternoon. "My mother called today," she said, "—about my condominium." Renee Jarrett's best friend was a realtor who thought she had a potential buyer for the property.

"What about the condo?" Sean toddled up to the coffee table and Greg shifted his beer bottle out of the tot's reach and handed him a toy fire engine.

"She was wondering when I was going to empty it and transfer my things out here."

"Makes sense...if you feel ready."

"No point in holding on to the space—is there?"

"Nope." Privately Greg felt it was a great idea that Jane wanted to cut that tie. "Say, this might be a good time for all of us to go to Dallas. Take the kids to meet their Jarrett relatives."

Jane hadn't expected this complication. It would have been so easy to explain about the sale of one unit, but how would Greg react on discovering the transaction included the entire complex, which she also happened to own? One explanation would merely lead to another, and another. *This web I've woven gets more tangled every day.* But the time wasn't ripe for the untangling yet.

"Well, actually, it wouldn't," she said. "I'll be busy...packing...sorting...the twins would be underfoot and besides, we'd barely have a chance to visit. If you can do without me for a couple of days, it'd be better to get this move out of the way, then all of us could go down later on."

Greg's antennae raised. Jane was uncomfortable about something. What? Here he'd spent the day envisioning...envisioning who knows what, while she'd been making plans to return to Dallas. Alone. Since the wedding, he'd stopped agonizing that she might leave. Now the possibility hit him between the eyes again and it angered him. She might be talking a couple of days there, but... "Are you sure you're not rushing?—moving everything?"

"You just said it makes sense."

"Then I take it back. Maybe you should give yourself a little more time."

"Are you saying what I think you're saying?" Jane answered with a steely glare.

"I know you love the kids," he said.

"But in spite of that love I might desert them? Your faith in me is touching."

"Then don't act like you can't wait to get away from us. Being homesick's an honest emotion, though. It wouldn't be a crime to admit you feel a need to touch base."

"*This* is my home, remember? Just because I mentioned a fast trip to Dallas doesn't mean I want to stay there. But I can't abandon my property to the care of others. And I'm the only one who can determine what possessions need to go where. I probably should have seen to it before we married, but the wedding was so rushed." *And I was afraid if I left, you might change your mind about us again.*

"Well, go whenever you like. I'm sure Nita will help out here. I can always depend on her."

Unlike me? Jane wanted to ask. No wonder Greg was having such a hard time loving her. He hadn't gotten around to trusting her yet. And now it sounded as if he couldn't care less about her going, or whether she'd ever come back.

Greg wiped the perspiration from his eyes and looked at his watch. *She's been gone twenty-six hours.* It still rankled that she didn't want the three of them to come along even though it did make sense that she couldn't accomplish much with two babies in tow. However, the fact of her going alone heightened his fears that once there she'd realize all she'd been giving up.

He tried to tell himself that the worry was because of the children. They'd already lost one mother; it wasn't fair they lose another. What he hadn't anticipated was that he would miss her so much. Only a day gone and he felt as if a part of himself had vanished with her.

He tried to keep such thoughts at bay with chores, letting Nita stay with the children while he opted for hard manual ranch labor. Branding, vaccinating, a last haying to offset the risk of early frost. He hoped the rigorous activity would drain all his energy and attention. And it helped some—during the day.

However, once night had fallen, the sleeping babies upstairs, Greg felt more alone than ever. And although tired of body, his mind was restless.

If he were a hard-drinking man, downing a bottle of eighty-proof bourbon would be just the ticket right now—numbing his inner turmoil by getting rip-roaring drunk. But Greg didn't have the luxury of escaping into a bottle. The children might need him.

The third day of Jane's absence was just as long and lonely as the others. Greg entertained the notion of phoning her...no, she might conclude he was checking up on her. He didn't want to come off as the jealous husband. Eventually, however, he gave in to temptation and placed the call, only to reach the answering machine at the condo. Greg felt like ramming a fist through the wall. That infernal machine was a menace—it had caused him problems before.

He thought back to those unanswered calls regarding the ad, how he'd almost given up on Jane before she'd picked up at the last minute of his last try. He had come within a few seconds of not meeting her at all. Of never having had her in his life. *Stop this!*

Maybe she's at her parents, he reasoned. He picked up the receiver then slammed it back down. *If she wants to talk to me, she can damn well phone here.* He needed to resign himself to the fact that Jane would either return tomorrow as promised or she wouldn't, and probably nothing he said or did would alter that decision. *But you'd think she would ring to check on the babies.* Unless, once in her natural setting, she didn't care about any of them anymore.

Darkness had erased everything but the well-lit house when Jane turned into the Circle G driveway late that same night. Determined to be back as soon as possible, she'd amazed even herself by accomplishing so much so quickly. To that end, she'd moved like a whirling dervish. Realtor meetings resulted in a fast sell to a corporate buyer, leaving Jane free for packing, tagging furniture and on-the-run visits with family members.

When tempted to call to the ranch, she resisted. Calls weren't necessary—the babies were in good hands. Getting home without delay was the important thing. And maybe, just maybe, her absence might have made a difference to Greg, that is if he got over his sulks and noticed her being gone.

She opened the car door and stared into the overflowing back seat of the BMW. Items she considered necessities—clothing, family pictures, important documents—plus gifts for the babies, Elton and Nita, and even Greg were crammed there. The rest of her belongings would be packed by a moving company, some to be shipped to the ranch, the rest parceled out to her family or donated to a women's shelter.

Her mother had volunteered to oversee the movers and cleaning crew and arrange disconnecting the telephone. All that was left for Jane to do was invest the profits she'd made on the condo deal, some of which would be paid to her immediately in the form of a tidy down payment, the rest to be paid quarterly for the next ten years.

Although disappointed that Greg and the twins weren't with her, the visit—frantic though it was—had mollified her family somewhat. Especially Jane's mention that she'd return soon, bringing Greg and the children.

Still brooding, Greg was pacing the kitchen floor when he heard the car and rushed to see who it was. His heart was beating in double-time when he opened the door and spied Jane. He took a deep gulp of air and exhaled before speaking out. "So, you came back," he said, shooting for a tone of casualness and trying to hide the relief that washed over him.

"As fast as I could," Jane answered. "Just like I said." She gazed up at him. "I hope you're glad to see me."

He didn't answer, but no words were needed. Greg walked silently toward her and lifted her off her feet as he wrapped her securely in his arms in a welcoming hug. He was squeezing the life out of her and his chin, stubbled at the end of the day, was scratching her face, but it felt wonderful. Jane's arms circled his neck as naturally as drawing a breath and she sighed happily against the collar of his shirt. She could have remained in his embrace for hours. If this was a typical Merrifield homecoming, perhaps she should go away more often.

Finally releasing her, Greg said, "The twins really missed you...and so did I. They're asleep but we can peek in if you'd like."

Arm in arm they tiptoed into the nursery. Jane stroked the cheeks of her children, hardly able to resist picking them up and cuddling each one. By now she'd had enough experience, however, to know that if she did, they'd be awake for half the night and cranky tomorrow. Not good. Besides, she needed time alone with their father.

He brought in her luggage and packages. "I thought you were clearing out the condo. Looks like you spent your time clearing out Dallas stores."

"Oh, I managed to get to one or two. Couldn't come home empty-handed."

He looked at one of the bags. "I see you even stopped by Neiman-Marcus. Having withdrawal pains?"

"Not anymore." She stole a quick kiss. "I'm glad we're teasing now instead of fussing."

"So am I," he answered, returning her kiss just as fleetingly. It was difficult for Greg to rein himself in, but he was determined to. If he really kissed Jane the way he wanted, this night wouldn't stop at mere kisses. And while that sounded rather nice, he'd made a decision that their first lovemaking would be nothing less than perfect.

That meant privacy. With the twins, there was always the possibility of interruption. What he planned to do was prevail on Elton and Nita to baby-sit, while he and Jane escaped on a honeymoon, a *real* honeymoon. Colorado Springs would be ideal. They could spend a weekend at the

Broadmoor. Total luxury, hot tubs and champagne. He'd show Jane how much he loved her. And hopefully, she'd respond by loving him just as much.

Greg grinned. He might have been a bit slow on the uptake, but just as Elton had surmised, Greg Merrifield intended to court his wife. To woo Jane until she never wanted to leave the Circle G without them again—not even for a brief trip to Dallas.

Before any wooing, however, the first step was to keep that appointment with his lawyer, finalize the legalities that had been hanging over him—Charlotte's will, insurance, all those details he'd avoided too long. He couldn't give Jane the attention she deserved until his past was well and truly behind him.

Greg stared out the window of the law office, dazed by Mike Murphy's words. The last thing he'd expected today was the news that he was immersed in a financial quagmire. He turned back to the attorney. "I don't understand, Mike. What do you mean there's no money?"

"Simple." Mike leaned forward on his elbows. "As you know, that insurance policy of Charlotte's was signed over to the funeral home."

Greg waved his hand dismissively. "That policy was peanuts. But the inheritance from her folks—?"

"Wasn't due to pass to her until age twenty-five."

Greg ruffled his forehead. "She died a few weeks

short of that birthday, but I just assumed everything came to me."

"It would have, except for the twins. There was a provision that if she passed on before inheriting, and left surviving children, then the trust would be held in abeyance for them until they're twenty-five. The only exception is college expenses. So Sean and Sarah are assured of money for their education, but nothing's available now."

Greg stared at the ceiling for several moments before looking at the attorney again. "Mike, I was depending on that money to pay off the Ibsen land purchase. The final note's coming due—a big note." Greg shook his head. "Charlotte's gone, I have acreage coming out the wazoo, and without her money, there's no way on earth I can make good on that dratted note."

"If I remember correctly the rest of your property is tied up in that deal, too." Mike fumbled with some file folders, grabbed a handful of papers and scanned the documents. "You pledged the other land in lieu of a down payment."

Greg nodded. "Creative financing. Smart, huh?"

"Don't beat up on yourself." He glanced up. "Maybe you can get an extension. The bank ought to understand."

"Mike, you're getting soft in the head. Banks aren't in the understanding business. Besides, that'd just be robbing Peter to pay Paul. I'm overextended as it is, what with Charlotte's medical expenses and all. Since I was counting on the inheritance, I hadn't given much thought to how deep a hole I'd dug.

I've even been expanding my herd, draining my cash reserves. I should have been minding my business, instead of—'' Greg ran his palm across his face and emitted a frustrated sigh. ''How could I have let myself get into such a jam? And aren't you supposed to protect me from self-destruction and stupidity?'' He gave Mike a rueful smile.

Mike patted his shoulder. ''Unfortunately I'm only brilliant, not clairvoyant.''

''When I think of the other expenses I have to consider—salaries, taxes, and those little necessities of life like food and diapers.'' Greg rubbed the back of his neck in frustration.

''I'm sorry, Greg. Wish I could do something.''

''Yeah. Me, too.''

''Needless to say, my bill's on hold for as long as you need.''

''Thanks, Mike.''

Even though he considered the effort useless, Greg did stop by the bank before he left Pampa. The reaction was as negative as he'd predicted.

''We can run your application by our underwriters, but frankly...'' The bank officer shook his head. ''Even if we could refinance, it'd be a monstrous monthly payment.''

His tone made Greg feel like a deadbeat begging for handout.

''I'm doubtful it can be done, all things considered,'' the banker continued discouragingly. ''Title problems on your land, for instance. You said probate of your late wife's will isn't complete.''

Thoroughly demoralized, Greg left the bank, fanciful thoughts of a romantic honeymoon with Jane obliterated. How could he consider trying to make her care for him as a husband when he didn't have a damn thing to offer her now?

CHAPTER EIGHT

THE aroma of peach cobbler, Greg's favorite dessert, wafted through the kitchen as Jane untied her apron. After checking on the children who were sitting quietly on the floor surrounded by toys, she hastily glanced at the mirror in the front hallway. Earlier, she'd showered and dressed in a scoop-necked, sleeveless blouse and short shorts—one of the outfits she'd brought from Dallas, an outfit designed to catch Greg's eye. Makeup perfect, hair fluffed, Jane sat down to wait.

Shortly before six, she heard him pull into the driveway. Rushing to meet him at the door, all the greeting Jane got was a hasty "hello" before Greg disappeared into his bedroom to change clothes. When he came back down, he barely glanced her way before heading outside.

From the kitchen window she could see him at the corral, his arms propped against the top railing as he watched a mare and her colt penned there. The droop of his shoulders and the look of dejection on his face alarmed her.

Where he'd been all afternoon and why, Jane didn't know. But it had to be somewhere important because he'd worn his best sport shirt and new Dockers instead of jeans and work shirt. She distinctly remembered his attitude as he left, somewhat preoccupied, but also cheery, buoyant. After their reunion last night and his chipper attitude today, she'd surmised that Greg's excursion involved something positive. Now, judging from his demeanor, Jane knew his mission hadn't worked out as expected.

An hour passed. Jane fed the children and kept tabs on Greg through the window. He remained in the same spot, obviously lost in thought. During that time, she'd vacillated on whether to go to him or simply wait him out.

Well, she'd waited long enough. Gathering the twins in her arms, Jane started for the corral. Carrying both of them was a chore now since they were growing heavier, but she didn't like leaving the children alone in the house, even for the few seconds it would take to run across the yard. So carry it had to be.

From the bottom of the porch she called to Greg. He waved an answering hand and walked to meet her, taking Sean from her arms, but saying little. Jane's anxiety intensified. Greg was always animated with his children. Today he was practically mute. "Are you hungry?" she asked as they headed back into the house.

"Not yet. If you don't mind, I think I'll take a drive." He sat Sean in the playpen, then left the three of them to their own devices. He didn't say where he was going or when he'd be back and somehow Jane sensed it was better to let him be.

After Greg left, she gave the twins a bath and read bedtime stories before tucking them into their cribs. Downstairs again, she sat in Greg's overstuffed recliner and turned on the television, low enough to pick up any baby whimpers from the portable monitor and to ensure she heard Greg when he came in.

Shortly after eleven the back door creaked. Jane listened as the refrigerator door opened and closed, then the microwave began its loud hum. She hesitated, building her nerve, before extricating herself from the soft recesses of the chair and entering the kitchen. Greg was hunched tiredly over the table, a near-empty milk glass and an untouched serving of brisket and grilled vegetables in front of him.

"What's wrong?" she said.

Greg's head snapped up in a double-take, but his composure wavered only for an instant. "What are you doing awake?" He looked toward a cow-shaped wall clock to verify the time, then asked, "Twins are okay, aren't they? You aren't up because of them?"

"No, I purposely waited for you. Don't you want to talk about what's bothering you?" She posed the question gently so as to avoid confrontation, yet was determined that Greg open up to her.

"Oh, it's just a trifle—not even worth discussing."

Jane wasn't deterred by Greg's evasiveness. His earlier actions and the sadness in his eyes said something traumatic had happened and she wanted to get to the bottom of it.

"Don't try to con me," she scolded, realizing the gentle routine was getting her nowhere. "We may not have been married long, but I'm tuned into you enough to spot something major going on."

"Oh, is that right?" A wary glance.

"Yes, that's right. Talk to me, Greg," she said pleadingly as she took a chair across from him.

"I don't feel much like talking." He pushed his plate away and crossed his arms on the table.

"Well, that's too bad, because I do."

"Angling for a fight?"

"No, not a fight, just some answers." Jane rose and came around to Greg's chair. She knelt down and faced him, steadying herself with a hand on his chair. "Whatever's wrong, level with me—like a husband to a wife. Don't distance yourself like this," she begged, rising to her feet.

"It's not that simple, Janie."

She didn't expect the familiar nickname, or the endearing way he said it. Temporarily at a loss for words, Jane paced the kitchen, finally stopping to turn his way. "Where *were* you today?"

Greg gave her a quick glance, then averted his eyes. She deserved an answer and he knew it. Only he hated to admit what a no-account he'd become. The last thing he wanted to do was lose face with Jane. He preferred to have a solution to the mess he was in before she knew the extent of it.

He rotated his shoulders, trying to work out the kinks. His neck was knotted from tension and he had a fierce headache. It wasn't talk he needed from Jane, it was comfort…he needed to be close to her, to have her massage his temples…to have her kiss all his troubles away— *You're losing it, man.*

"I was in my lawyer's office," he finally said. "Taking care of some business I should have handled months ago. Satisfied?" Hoping against hope that she was and that she'd call a halt to this interrogation, Greg picked up his plate and carried it to the sink, dumping the uneaten food into the disposal.

"No, I'm not satisfied," Jane responded. "Not until you explain why you're so on edge."

"I'm not on edge," Greg lied, "just bushed. It's been a long day. Can't we talk about this tomorrow?" He pulled a gallon jug of milk from the refrigerator and refilled his glass.

"But—" Jane started to protest, then realized that she had her answer. *Charlotte.* Greg had been to see his lawyer, to confer over something related to his first marriage. Now that Jane had that snippet of information, it didn't require much imagination to guess what was going on in Greg's mind.

Once more he was consumed with thoughts of his old life. That would be the reason for his malaise, the reason he wouldn't be forthright about it. And to think she'd believed they were moving forward.

"Like I said, we'll talk tomorrow. Good night." Glass of milk in hand, Greg left the kitchen and headed upstairs. Jane felt sick at heart.

Although she arose early the next morning, Greg wasn't there. Jane checked his room and found the bed rumpled, but still made. It appeared as if he'd only napped. He wasn't anywhere in the house and there were no signs of life outside, either, so she supposed he'd left to do chores.

It was late afternoon, the sun a shimmering orange ball on the horizon, when she saw him ride up to the corral and dismount. Despite her sister's romantic notion of a hero on horseback, it was rare to see Greg on a horse. Usually Elton's pickup or a four-wheel-drive vehicle served ranch purposes. Even last night, he'd gone for a drive in the van. So this ride must have been for exercise or for thinking.

Greg gave the reins to one of the hands and trotted toward the flagstone patio where Jane was sitting, keeping watch while the children played in a small inflated baby pool.

Sean and Sarah wore matching boy-girl red-striped swimsuits and were happily slapping the water and chewing on wet washcloths or dunking plastic boats. Greg bent over to kiss each baby on the head. "Da," Sarah gurgled. Sean started climbing over the edge and Greg plopped him back into the plastic pool, handing him a rubber duck for amusement.

"I'll get us a beer," Greg announced, "then we can have that talk."

Jane felt queasy. Greg had apparently ridden out alone, using the hours of solitude to work out in his mind what to say to her. She wasn't sure she was ready to hear it. The possibility he wanted to call it quits suddenly loomed in her thoughts. What if he was primed to tell her the marriage was over?

Greg returned with two bottles of Budweiser in insulated liners. He sat in the patio chair next to hers and lifted his beer in the air as a toast. "Cheers."

Although she felt nothing approximating "cheer," nevertheless, Jane echoed Greg's toast and took a swallow of the cold brew to fortify herself.

"The meeting with Mike—my lawyer—was…" Greg began hesitantly, "difficult." He was talking to a spot behind Jane. "For reasons you can't possibly imagine." His gaze was still focused elsewhere as if he was formulating his message in his mind.

Jane waited for him to continue, but Greg remained silent, sipping his beer. She couldn't stand it any longer and finally broke the silence. "Please tell me before I explode. I need to know how this impacts us."

Now he looked directly at her, studying her long and hard before reaching over to lift her chin with his fingers. "Not in the way you may be thinking. I know Charlotte's gone to me forever. I've accepted the loss and I'm doing my best to get on with our life."

"You said *our*."

"They're one and the same as far as I'm concerned. At least they were until yesterday."

"What happened then?"

"I told you about buying the Ibsen place. Remember?"

Jane nodded.

"I didn't tell you everything. You see, Charlotte and I didn't have the money or resources to purchase it outright, but we just couldn't pass up the opportunity to link our folks' two ranches. So we went over to First Independent in Pampa and took out a big mortgage. We had such dreams. A bigger herd, more crops, too."

Greg paused to take another swig of beer. "It was a safe investment, or so I thought, even though we committed our other acreage instead of putting cash down. All we had to cover were a couple of annual interest-only payments, then a balloon note would come due, and before that happened...

"When Charlotte's parents died." Greg backtracked. "The majority of their estate passed directly to her—their land, personal effects and so on. Most of the liquid assets...money, bonds, life insurance...were tied up in a trust fund due to mature when she reached twenty-five. We planned to use those assets for the balloon payment. Seemed simple and risk-free..."

"But?"

"Charlotte didn't live to see that twenty-fifth birthday." Once more he gazed off into the distance, as if cursing the fates. Eventually he faced Jane again. "I didn't give the trust a thought at the time. I was too consumed with..."

"With grief?"

"Yes. And with seeing to Sean and Sarah. To say nothing of carrying out Charlotte's last wish." He paused a moment. "That done, I moved on to other things. The twins were happy. You seemed to be adjusting to ranch life and I was sort of bobbing along, going with the flow. Getting this legal stuff out of the way was the last hurdle in putting the past totally behind me. I swear to you, Jane, I was even looking forward to getting all this over and done with."

Greg thought about his next plans, the courtship he'd plotted. *Yeah, right.* What would Jane think about being courted by a good-for-nothing like him? Vowing to support her and now literally faced with losing the farm.

"So what happened to the trust?"

"It's passed on to the twins, not to be touched until *they're* twenty-five. Unless they need some for college."

Greg hung his hands between his knees and stared down at the patio floor. "Jane, I can't meet that balloon note. I've been hoping for some sort of brainstorm, but there hasn't been one. Frankly, I don't know what I'm going to do."

"What *we're* going to do," she reminded him.

"It isn't fair to saddle you with this."

"Whoever said life was fair? We're living proof that sometimes it isn't."

"But to have you fall victim to my...my... I didn't make many commitments to you, but I said I'd take care of you and now...now I'm faced with bailing out." He rubbed the back of his neck. "What I'm trying to say is that if you want to bail out, too, then—"

"Bailing out? Divorce? Is that what this conversation is about?" Her raised voice caught the babies' attention and Sarah's lips curled downward. Jane rose to comfort her. Seated once more, she turned to Greg, her voice quiet, level. "Is that what you want?"

He didn't answer.

"I repeat, is that what you want? Just because you've had a share of bad luck, you're—"

"A share?" Greg interrupted. "I seem to have cornered the market on that commodity."

"My, my. On a regular pity party, aren't we?" Jane retorted. "How about an answer, though? Is all this about a divorce?" Her no-nonsense tone demanded a response.

"From the onset I told you this marriage was forever. Sean and Sarah are attached to you. I'd sooner be drawn and quartered than deprive them—" Greg sighed. "Things have changed, though. I was just trying to give you an easy out."

"How magnanimous," Jane hissed. "Problem is, I don't *want* out." She glanced at the children, once more splashing happily.

"I have no intention of leaving *my* children," she announced, looking Greg straight in the eyes. "I'm not budging. Unless you want to give me custody, that is."

Greg bounded to his feet.

"I thought not," Jane said knowingly as his dark gaze told her precisely what he thought of that idea. "So I suggest we stop wasting valuable time and use our energies for figuring out a solution."

Despite Greg's offer of freedom, Jane could see relief written on his face—he didn't want her to leave; it was male bravado spurring him on. Greg might think he'd married her only as a mother for his children, but while she continued filling that role, there was hope for something more. "So all that's bothering you is money?" she asked.

Greg leaned back his head and groaned. "Yeah," he said sarcastically, "just money. Oh, that and keeping a roof over our heads since I don't have enough."

"Perhaps this isn't as much of a hurdle as you think. I can help."

"If you're envisioning us doing a Bonnie and Clyde routine, forget it. Armed robbery isn't my thing."

"No, armed robbery wasn't what I had in mind." Jane forced a small laugh, then drew in a breath. This wasn't the way she'd planned to tell him, but she couldn't let her own insecurities interfere with something this important. "Greg," she said, "I have money."

"Forget it." He gave her a look that said *I'm not going to touch your little piggy bank.* "I will not start off a marriage by draining my wife's savings."

His concern about her savings was sweet, but unwarranted. Jane had modeled since age thirteen and the prudent investments of an astute business manager meant she had significant resources at her disposal. And there was that chunk of cash from the condo down payment, too. "Don't be so chauvinistic. It's my money. I ought to be able to spend it any way I see fit."

"Save your breath. I will not take your nest egg."

"A marriage is a partnership. Let—"

"Drop it, Jane."

"But we can't lose the ranch." She shook her head. *Just listen to me, I sound like the hand-wringing heroine in an old Western.*

"Give me a few days and I'll think of something." Greg didn't sound all that confident.

"But you just admitted that no ideas have come to you. Let's tackle this—"

He cut her off once more. ''The subject is closed. I'll let you know when I've figured out how to handle things.'' He stood up.

''This conversation isn't over,'' Jane threatened.

''Yes, it is.'' His mouth was pressed into a straight line. Then it softened. ''Look, Jane. I appreciate your wanting to pitch in, but this is a muddle I created and I've got to find my own way out.''

Jane felt like slapping him silly for being so obstinate, but at the moment he needed encouragement more than abuse. ''Exactly how much would I have to come up with?''

''Boy, you don't give up, do you? Okay, Lady Bountiful, it's two hundred and fifty thousand dollars—that's a cool quarter of a million. Now do you understand? Your contribution wouldn't make a dent.''

If you only knew. ''Ohh, I see…'' Jane muttered, letting him think she was taken aback by the amount. True, it was a lot of money to raise on the spur-of-the-moment, but funds she could easily come by.

The stumbling block, however, was Greg. Jane had struck a nerve, a macho stubbornness that would probably rebuff any offer from her, even if he knew she had it to spare. As he said, he considered this *his* problem, not hers, not theirs. *Okay, be mulish,* she thought. She was simply going to have to take matters into her own hands.

When Jane got up the next morning, she could hardly wait to push Greg out the door. Yet he seemed in no hurry, dawdling over breakfast,

spending a good hour in his office. It wasn't until
Elton stopped by that he finally left. The minute her
privacy was assured, Jane called Sid Snyder, her
business manager.

"That's right, Sid, two hundred and fifty thousand." Jane instructed him to contact an officer at
the bank in Pampa and arrange for the transfer immediately. She wanted a Paid In Full on Greg's note
before Sid broke for lunch. "I don't care how—just
do it. The money's there as you well know. Start
with the cash from the condo, tap my savings,
liquidate some stocks or certificates of deposit, do
whatever you need to—"

"There'll be a penalty if we go to the CD's,"
Sid said. "You might take a hit on the stocks, too.
Extra taxes and all."

"Sid, you know good and well I can afford any
penalties or taxes."

"Are you sure you want to do this?" His tone
was leery.

Jane was fed up. First Greg, now Sid treating her
like a ten-year-old who didn't know her own mind.
"I'm a grown woman, Sid. I earned the money and
I can do whatever I choose with it."

"No offense, Jane. I didn't mean to insinuate—"

"It's okay." Jane interrupted. "Just get this
taken care of. As soon as possible, please."

Within the hour, Sid called back informing her
dryly that "the deed is done." Now what Jane had
to get through was Greg's reaction. She'd acknowledge her meddling—and all the other nuggets of
information she'd withheld—when he came in for
supper. Not likely to be a pretty scene.

Hoping a special meal and a bottle of wine might mellow him, put him in a better frame of mind to accept her disclosures, Jane started to the kitchen to see what kind of food the freezer and pantry held—specifically comfort food designed for mellowing husbands.

Jane was removing steamy baked lasagna from the oven when Greg walked into the kitchen that evening. "Hello," he said, ignoring the fancy table setting and the pungent vapors filling the room. He silently took a seat at the kitchen table and carefully crossed one leg atop the other. The expression he wore was unreadable, a perfect poker face.

"Hello yourself," Jane answered, glancing around from the stove. She didn't like this. Something was amiss. Greg had an unnatural calmness about him, the same kind of eerie stillness that can precede an oncoming tornado.

He knows. He'd found out what she had done and was maintaining a facade of composure, biding his time before erupting. "Would you like some wine?" she asked warily, handing him a corkscrew. A bottle of Cabernet Sauvignon and two stemmed glasses were already on the table.

"Sean and Sarah asleep?" He opened the wine and handed Jane a glass.

"They were tired. Helga came out to see them this afternoon and they missed their nap." She set her wine on the cabinet and proceeded to toss a salad with a nervous vigor as she kept Greg in her line of vision.

"You've had a busy day," he said, his teeth showing in a preternatural grin.

"Not much more than usual. Except for Helga's visit. Her husband's really on the mend." Jane kept up the tossing, her nervousness increasing.

"That's nice." One set of Greg's fingers was now beating a tattoo on the table.

Jane couldn't bear this waiting. She turned around. "Is there something on your mind?"

"You might say that." The stormy expression he now wore told her rough seas lay ahead. "I suppose you're waiting for some inane comment like 'Oh, goodness gracious, where did you get all the money?'"

His accusatory look was met with one of dismay. From the minute she'd decided on her course of action, Jane had been apprehensive. And it wasn't as if she expected Greg to be grateful—not at first, anyway. He had an abundance of pride and she knew up-front that she would be tromping all over it. But pride aside, she had hoped Greg would be so relieved to be off the hook that he'd forgive her for going against his expressed wishes.

Instead there was only coldness in his eyes. "How long did you think you could keep up the lie? Maybe you consider me some dumb as dirt cowboy," he snarled, "but I'm not. At least not anymore." He stood up and pulled a magazine from his back pocket, then flung it on the kitchen counter. It was opened to a big glossy picture of her.

CHAPTER NINE

"You lied to me. Told me you were in advertising, let me think you were a secretary, assistant...what have you. And here you are—a big-time model." Greg jabbed at the ad with his forefinger. "J.J. is it?"

"Yes, J.J." The nickname seemed almost alien to her now.

"I can see it all. Just like Clark Kent becomes Superman, with a wave of the wand, Jane Jarrett transforms into 'J.J., Supermodel.'"

"Clark Kent doesn't use a wand," she said witlessly. "Last TV show I watched he spun around in a circle."

"Don't try to get me off the subject. We were talking about you and *your* secret identity." Greg wrapped his hands around the top rung of the ladder-back kitchen chair and frowned her way.

"All right, so I didn't tell the whole truth. But modeling's part of my past, a part that's no longer important."

"Important enough to generate funds for a huge financial rescue." Greg sat back down at the table and hooked a booted foot on his chair's bottom rim. "Why didn't you tell me?"

"Because I knew you'd respond exactly this way."

"If you think that justifies misleading me the whole time—"

"I'm not trying to justify anything, I'm just attempting to explain. How did you find out?"

"About which part? The financial rescue? Or the fact that pictures of my wife are sold at checkout counters and newsstands from here to Kalamazoo?"

"Quit making it sound like something disreputable—like I'm some kind of porno queen."

"I didn't insinuate anything of the kind." His eyes narrowed. "You haven't done any of *that* sort of posing, have you?"

Jane stormed over to the table and slammed down the salad bowl. Lettuce, tomatoes and cucumber slices flew out onto the linen cloth. "Just because I stepped on your sensibilities doesn't give you a right to be offensive."

Greg shrugged. "Guess not."

"You still haven't told me how you found out."

"Stumbled into it." Carefully, Greg picked up his glass, examined the contents, then sipped the wine, as Jane waited impatiently for more information. She wanted to signal him to hurry up, but she knew Greg wasn't going to be hurried. He was determined to extract his pound of flesh slowly, very slowly.

"I told you I could solve my problem on my own and I was in the process of doing it," he continued about the time Jane was ready to scream. "I didn't need you to take over."

"Oh? Last time I heard, you didn't have a solution. It would have been nice if you'd clued me in.''

''I would have, but while I was getting my act together, you'd already charged in like one of the Texas Rangers—as I discovered secondhand.''

''Why don't you omit the colorful asides and lay it all out in sequence.''

''Be glad to. First thing I did was talk to Elton who chewed me out for not coming to him immediately. Then after agreeing with me that I'd been pretty dumb, he gave me some advice, and offered a sizable personal loan—both of which I accepted.''

''So you're willing to take Elton's money, but not mine?''

''He offered a loan to my face, which I was going to make worth his while with generous interest. You snuck around behind my back and shelled out the whole amount as effortlessly as buying a hotel in a Monopoly game.''

''I tried talking about it and got the me-man you-woman routine.''

''That's because I didn't know I was dealing with someone as rich as the Queen of England.''

''No more snide remarks remember? Just tell me the rest.''

''Elton suggested I talk to the bank in Martinsville. Their loan department is real small…that's why I went to Pampa originally…but I know everyone at the Martinsville bank personally. Sometimes that makes a difference to a guy in a bind. Then I ran it by Mike, my lawyer, and he reminded me I could get a short-term loan on my retirement account also. If I hadn't been so panicky,

I probably would have come up with these options on my own. But for a while there, I was in a state of brainlock.

"Putting Elton's money with the retirement loan, then working out some kind of refinancing, I'd have bought myself a couple of months. By then, the will would have been probated, giving me the flexibility to sell some of the land if necessary."

"So you went to the bank in Martinsville?"

"Yep. Right after talking with Elton and Mike, And lo and behold, Ralph, the head honcho there, thought we could work something out. So, first order of business was phoning the bank in Pampa to get the payoff amount. Imagine our shock to learn 'Mrs. Merrifield's business manager handled that about half an hour ago'—the balance was zeroed out."

He gave her a frosty stare. "So I had to sit there wearing a possum-eating grin and spewing inanities about 'ha ha' my wife beating me to the punch, while trying to pretend I wasn't in total shock. And all the time Ralph was congratulating me on my marriage and asking to meet that 'enterprising little wife' of mine."

Jane slumped down at the table and gulped her wine. This was worse than she'd imagined.

"It took a little sleuthing on my own to figure out how you acquired that quarter mil you plunked down on my behalf. So happens my old college roommate lives in Dallas. Ryan Williams. He's the anchor on one of the evening news broadcasts. And glory be, not only had he heard of you, but he tells me you know each other."

"Yes, we've met," Jane said. "I've run across him at several media functions."

"Small world." Greg refilled his own glass of wine.

Too darn small.

"So did you think you could keep me in the dark forever, with a zillion people knowing your face?"

"No, but if I'd told you right off about my career, you'd have brushed me off like lint."

"Damn straight. Immediately after getting your autograph of course."

"So where'd you locate the old magazine?"

"Florine's Beauty Salon. When I left the bank, I walked over there and browsed through all her old magazines. Had to fight off Florine who wanted to trim my hair. Needless to say, her clientele were tickled about this new interest of mine and why I kept staring at the Carvel ads. I'm sure that by now they've put two and two together. Did you think Martinsville women are so backward they have no interest in style or don't know who's who?"

"I've never even so much as hinted at such a thing. You're the one who seems to have the hang-up about small-town limitations."

"Forget my hang-ups. We're talking about you and your deceit." He got up and grabbed the magazine from the counter, tossing it back down on the table in front of Jane. "There are a slew of others out in the van—*Cosmopolitan, Good Housekeeping, Mademoiselle,* to name a few. "Every single one has an article—or at least a full-page ad—on the Carvel Woman. *You...* decked out in silks, sequins and a ton of makeup. Enough pictures to fill the walls at the National Gallery, to say nothing of a thousand billboards. I don't know what bothers me more—to discover I've been so blindly stupid or that my wife is such a fraud.''

"I was intending to tell you tonight.''

"Right.'' Greg picked up the wine bottle and examined the label. "Nice brand…and this—'' he gestured around the room—at the fresh flowers she'd brought in from the garden, their best china. "Was all this supposed to help soften me up while you finally owned up to everything?''

Jane ignored the gibe. "I did what I thought was necessary to stay in your life. To become Sean's and Sarah's mother.''

"In other words, the end justified the means. Think again,'' Greg growled. "You should have told me regardless of the consequences. So what happens the next time truth doesn't serve your purposes?''

"There won't be a next time, Greg. No more subterfuge, I promise. And I don't take promises lightly, either.''

He stroked his chin as if wondering whether he could truly trust her. "And what about our other issue—your compulsion to pull my bacon out of the fire? I realize that for you two hundred and fifty thousand dollars is chump change. According to this article—'' he grabbed the magazine and waved it "—you make more in one hour than I clear in a week. But I'd just as soon you'd let me handle my predicament by myself.''

"I considered the possibility of losing the Circle

G to be *our* predicament. I live here, too. I thought it was supposed to be my home.''

''For now anyway. Until the new wears off and you begin missing your adoring public. Then you'll start having second thoughts and...'' Greg stopped himself. She'd snookered him—that's for sure—but he'd protect a smidgen of his pride by never letting her know how badly it stung. ''I should have listened to my instincts on this. I damn sure should have checked you out instead of marrying you on faith.''

''Maybe so, but we *are* married. And as far as your so-called faith is concerned, if I'm tiring of the ranch, then why did I make such a hefty investment in the place only this morning?''

''How the hell am I supposed to know why you do what you do? I haven't exactly had a lot of experience with rich glamour girls.''

Jane reached up and touched his arm. ''Give me half a chance and we can work through this.''

For a moment Jane thought she'd convinced him. He stood immobile, staring down into her eyes as though he were contemplating pulling her into his arms, then drew back. ''Can we? I hardly see this *kept-man* position you've placed me in as a basis for working through anything.''

Strong words, yet that was exactly how Greg felt. He'd had plenty of concerns about their forging a union, but finances hadn't been one of them. He knew Jane wasn't in dire need of money. It was evident she'd had exposure to the finer things in life, but he'd chalked that up to her belonging to a well-off family. Still he'd always thought he could hold his own and give her what she was used to.

He'd never dreamed she was a celebrity with un-imagined wealth at her fingertips, a supermodel at that. Even now it was hard to match those sleek magazine photos with the woman he'd married. But yes, the face was the same. Just with a bit more makeup and minus the glasses that Jane—myopic as could be—depended on when she removed her contacts.

He'd done exactly what he'd warned himself not to do. He'd fallen for her. He should have known better than to begin dwelling on happy endings. Hadn't he once told Jane there was no such thing? The problem was, Greg hadn't been listening to himself. But now the message had been pounded into his head with the force of a sledgehammer. And it hurt like hell.

"So what do we do now?" Jane asked softly.

"Damned if I know."

"Then allow me to tell you. We move on. Like it or not, you no longer have to worry about losing the ranch. So we can start concentrating on *us*, on—"

"I'll add 'moving on' and 'concentrating' to my To Do list," Greg interrupted sarcastically.

Jane sighed. She could see there weren't going to be any concessions by Greg in the immediate future. "Would you like some supper now?"

"So solicitous. Downright wifely, in fact. But I'm not very hungry. Go ahead, eat. I'll be doing paperwork."

He left the room. Jane rose, taking a couple of

steps after him, then faltered. What could she say that she hadn't already said? Maybe tomorrow Greg would be more reasonable. She began putting the uneaten meal away. Like Greg her appetite was gone.

They might have been in the same house, but communication between Jane and Greg the next day was almost nonexistent. Not that he was purposely avoiding her. Rather than pursuing his usual ranch labor, he stayed inside, committing his energies to the office, sorting files, cleaning shelves. During his forays to other parts of the house, he seemed to be watching her, evaluating her, but never putting himself out to converse. When Jane spoke or asked questions, she received monosyllabic responses.

She'd left the twins in their playpen while she soaked hand-washables in the basin, and when she returned to the hallway, Greg's voice could be heard coming from the family room. He might be angry with her, but now there was no trace of rancor in his soft, gentle tone. Intrigued, she tiptoed closer and peeked around the corner.

Greg sat on the big leather couch with a baby in each arm, crooning to them in singsong fashion. "When you're bigger, I'll get you ponies. Pintos maybe. Would you like that?" Both babies stared up at him with adoring smiles.

Jane stood in the doorway, her heart warming to the tender scene. In her whole life, she'd never seen anything as glorious as that man cuddling his children. Jane was determined not to lose this. She could abide Greg's ire and sullenness—eventually he'd tire of his snit and recognize she'd done what she thought had to be done. *But will he ever love me?* Jane knew she would never stop wishing that he would.

When Greg raised his eyes from the children and noticed her standing there, his smile faded. The implicit message told Jane this storm was going to take a while to blow over.

The next two days proved her right. Greg was better at nursing a grudge than accepting apologies. Jane had underestimated his ability to stay mad and overestimated her ability to tolerate his behavior.

After seventy-two hours of Greg's silent treatment, she'd had it. Once the babies were asleep for the night, she stalked into the family room where Greg sat doing a crossword puzzle.

"Is this how a man acts when he feels his manhood threatened?"

His eyes lifted from the puzzle. "What's that crack supposed to mean?"

Well at least I got his attention. "Only that you're reacting to my money like you've been emasculated. If I had known it was going to cause this much discord, I'd have arranged for the loan to be paid by an *anonymous male benefactor.*"

"Oh, yeah. Like I believe in anonymous benefactors—male or female."

Jane was weary of his bitter cynicism. "You don't believe in anyone, do you Greg?—other than Elton or Charlotte, that is."

"Leave Charlotte out of it. This is only about you and me."

"Not so. You were willing to make use of her inheritance to pay off the loan, but—"

"That was different."

"Oh? Care to explain how?"

"Okay—since you're so set on debating it. With Charlotte, the land wasn't solely mine, it was hers, too. And buying the Ibsen property was a mutual decision."

"Is that what's bugging you?—the arrangement wasn't mutual? Well, *we* could have made a mutual decision if you'd let me in on it. You've been so self-righteous about my secrets, what about your own? I'd say hiding a major financial commitment, even a prior commitment, is pretty darn sneaky. So while you're wallowing in all that piousness, just keep in mind glass houses and stones." Leaving in a huff, Jane stormed upstairs.

For the next thirty minutes she lay on the bed, big wads of tissues in her hands to blot the flowing tears. *What now?* Jane knew this impasse couldn't continue indefinitely. Was there nothing she could do to get Greg off his high horse? This strained environment wasn't good for Sean and Sarah. To say nothing of the effect it was having on her. She'd cried more in the last several days than she had in the last year—and she'd shed more than a few tears over that time. Yet she didn't know how to make things right. It was too late to rectify the damage that was already done. She, Greg and the children just had to move on.

No longer crying, she was staring at the shadows on the ceiling when Greg opened the door an hour later. "What's your problem?"

Talk about asinine questions. She sat up, glad that the room was dim, the only lighting coming from the fixture in the hallway. Red, puffy eyes were too revealing. "Merely keeping myself removed from the field of battle." She was in no mood to continue the warfare, but she wasn't completely spiritless, either. If Greg wanted to fight some more, then by golly, they'd fight.

He came inside. "Don't you think it's time we discussed this rationally."

Too irritated to be self-conscious about her tear-stained face, Jane switched on the bedside lamp. "That takes two! I can't believe you're accusing me of being the irrational one."

Greg crossed the room and sat down beside her, a finger stroking her cheek. "I thought about what you said...you're right. I should have told you about the note, about my financial obligations. Should have told you before we married. And, however I've acted, I do appreciate being delivered from foreclosure."

Jane jerked away from his touch. "Under the circumstances that statement isn't at all credible."

"Well, I just didn't like having money bestowed on me without my knowledge. It may take the next thirty years, but I'll pay you back every penny of that loan."

"Darn your hide, Greg Merrifield. It *wasn't* a loan. Can't you get that through your thick skull? I don't want to be repaid. I wasn't trying to foist money on you—all I was trying to do was save our home."

Greg ran his hand through his hair as if trying to figure out what to do next.

"I hardly thought a man who'd advertise for a wife would be so prideful."

"This is about more than pride," he countered.

"The heck it is."

Greg took her hand. "So what do you think it's about?"

"Our marriage, that's what." Jane had been willing to let matters hang, to give him wide berth, but now that Greg had invaded her space they might as well get to the crux of the problem.

"You want out?" Greg's voice was pained.

"No. Am I being evicted?" Jane's voice was equally distressed.

Before he could respond, the telephone rang. He picked up the receiver, then passed it to Jane. "It's for you."

"Oh, hi!" Jane's eyes widened. Thrown off balance by the news, she could only mumble, "You are...when? Uh, sure...see you then."

A dial tone buzzed from the receiver dangling in Jane's hand. She looked at Greg. "My parents. They'll be here around noon tomorrow."

"We decided if the mountain won't come to Mohammed..." Jim Jarrett said with a chuckle, as he patted Greg on the back. "Did our phone call surprise you, Janie?"

If you only knew, Jane thought, still nonplussed that her mother and father were standing on the front porch of the Circle G.

"She was surprised, but delighted," Greg broke

in. "She's been looking for a good date for us to meet."

"We wanted to give you time to honeymoon before we intruded, but I simply couldn't wait a minute longer before getting acquainted with my new son-in-law and grandchildren," Renee said.

"Then we'd better go inside," Jane managed to say, her voice only slightly better than a squeak.

To Jane the next eight hours dragged on like eight years. As soon as she'd told him about the visit last night, Greg had put their quarrel on hold. And today he'd turned into another person, obviously intent on charming Jim and Renee and being totally successful. He gave them a tour of the Circle G, introduced them to Elton and Nita, and acted the besotted husband to their daughter.

The Jarretts fawned so enthusiastically over Sean and Sarah that a stranger would have imagined the twins were blood relatives of the Jarrett family. It was clear there would never be a "step" grandparent relationship with Jim or Renee.

Jane motioned toward the stuffed animals, blocks and picture books that littered the floor around Sean and Sarah. "Did you buy out a toy store before leaving Dallas?"

"You know your dad and his grandchildren." Renee took Jane's hand in hers. "I was a little apprehensive about barging in on you uninvited, but we just had to know whether you were really happy. The only way to do that was by spending a little time with you two. It's such a relief to see what a good pair you make." Renee reached across to pat Greg's hand, too.

Jane forced a smile. She didn't feel a bit happy at the moment. She felt like a nervous wreck. And it would only get worse. Entertaining her parents during the day was one thing, but now it was bedtime. Newlyweds with separate bedrooms? The marriage might not appear so idyllic to Jim and Renee after all.

All four adults were tucking the children in, the babies cranky from being spoiled, pampered and played with all day long. "Even when they're fussy, they're such delights," Renee said, helping Sarah into pajamas decorated with Sesame Street characters.

After kisses all around, the adults went back downstairs. "Why don't we crack open that champagne we brought and toast your future," Jane's father suggested.

"Sure thing," Greg said. "And I want to say thanks for the thoughtful gesture. I imagine you were skeptical about us, about—"

"True." Jim interrupted with a good-natured laugh. "Parents are protective, as you two are already learning. But Janie has a light in her eyes when she looks at you, a light I've never seen before. All we've ever wanted is for our daughter to be married to a good man, to be content. Now we know she is."

"I appreciate that, Jim. And I promise to do my best to see that she never regrets marrying me. Now I'd better fetch that champagne. Will you help me, darling?"

Jane hadn't heard that endearment from Greg before and though she realized it was more for her parents' benefit than hers, still the "darling" did sound wonderful.

Greg pulled the champagne bottle from the refrigerator while Jane retrieved flutes from the china cabinet. "Thanks for being so great about this," she said, watching him pop the cork and pour the bubbling liquid. They were heading back toward the den, when Jane stopped him. "Greg, there's something else." Jane didn't know quite how to say what was on her mind but she couldn't delay the conversation any longer. This might be her only chance to talk with Greg in private. "I wouldn't mention it except…except my parents would never understand and…and—"

"Are you asking to sleep in my bed?" There was an amused expression on his face.

This was not the time for levity. The quandary they were in wasn't funny—not to her anyway. "I can't very well stay in *my* room, now can I? Surely you can see that. So stop your gloating."

"Well, now, I don't know," Greg said thoughtfully. "Gloating feels pretty good. Maybe I should demand a little groveling from you, too." He nonchalantly examined the play of bubbles in the flutes while she fumed.

"Do you want me down on my knees?" she grumbled.

"No, I guess seeing you flustered like this is reward enough." He grinned again. "Shall I distract our visitors while you sneak your pj's and toothbrush down the hall?"

"Please," Jane said with relief, a weak smile on her lips. She had no choice but to let Greg have his fun with this. He'd agreed to go along with her request, to help her save face. At the moment, that was all that was important.

"On second thought," Greg added mischievously, "forget the pj's. You won't need them."

When Jane's mouth gaped open, he chuckled.

She gritted her teeth. "You're a million laughs tonight."

"Then all joking aside." He set the tray down and took Jane's shoulders in his hands. "Just know this...once you're in my bed, Jane, you're there for good. There'll be no carrying your stuff out when we see your folks' car headed back toward Dallas. The move is permanent."

CHAPTER TEN

WHEN everyone else said good-night, Jane lingered in the kitchen, adding detergent and starting the dishwasher, sponging off the cabinet fronts. Realizing she could no longer delay the inevitable, she switched off the lights and started upstairs.

After checking on the twins, Jane slipped inside Greg's bedroom, then leaned against the closed door, wondering what came next. The room had only one chair and Greg was sprawled in it, watching her movements as if he were a jungle animal, eyes all-seeing. He was shirtless, rippling muscles drawing Jane's gaze; his feet were bare, his belt loosened, the snap on his jeans undone. He looked relaxed—if there was any nervousness, it didn't show.

Should she go ahead and put on her nightclothes, or did he want to talk? If so, where did she sit? On the bed? Or should she simply rush across the room and throw herself in his lap? That would be a real icebreaker.

Greg took all the decisions out of her hands. With a fluid motion, he rose and ambled over to her, reaching behind her back to click the door's lock. Jane had been in Greg's bedroom before, but never with the two of them alone and never with the world beyond shut out this way. She felt fidgety, tingly, her pulse pounding in her ears.

He massaged her back, his fingertips moving skillfully and erotically along the length of her spine. She could feel his warm breath on her face, smell the mint of toothpaste and the citrus aroma of aftershave. Jane's mind registered that the room was dim, lighted only by the glow of several candles. He began kissing her…first her temples, then the plane of her cheek, then back to her ear before burying his face in her hair.

Greg's lovemaking sent flames of desire coursing through her. The passion between them that had been bubbling unchecked since that first meeting exploded like a volcano.

When his lips touched Jane's, Greg surrendered to the sensations that had hounded him mercilessly of late. His hands tangled in her marvelous hair— hair as soft as corn silk and smelling of strawberry shampoo. Her body fit right into his as naturally as two halves of a whole and he crushed even tighter against her as he savored what he'd been denying himself.

Why have I been fighting this? he wondered.

When her lips were freed from his, Jane whispered, "Why don't I get out of these clothes?"

"Good idea. I'll help."

"No, give me a minute. I, uh, need to brush my teeth."

"Okay, but hurry." He kissed her again.

Once in the bathroom, free of Greg's orbit, Jane's better judgment asserted itself. *Now* was no time for sex. There were too many unresolved issues. Why just yesterday they were bickering like schoolkids. Their argument hadn't been resolved, merely postponed because of her parents. A rush of embarrassment hit her. *My parents are here.* Covering her floral pajamas with a matching robe, she returned to the bedroom, determined to put a stop to Greg's seduction right this instant.

The sight of him sitting up in bed, a cotton sheet covering the lower half of his body, Wranglers crumpled on the floor, weakened her resolve. He beckoned her closer.

Jane sat on the edge of the bed. "We shouldn't…shouldn't be…" she protested.

"Shouldn't what?"

"You know. Doing this."

"I shouldn't be undressing you?" He tugged at the sash of her robe, untying it. "Shouldn't be kissing you?" He leaned closer, his mouth teasing Jane's lips. "This is exactly what we should be doing. For too long, I've wanted to hold you, love you."

He said "love." But does he mean love or have sex? At the moment, it ceased to matter. When Greg's hands pushed away the robe and strayed to the buttons of her pajamas, Jane tossed caution aside. She brought a hand to his face, cupping his chin in her palm and tracing a thumb across his lower lip as she dared to touch and caress him freely.

"My parents are here," she demurred, without conviction.

"At the opposite end of the hall."

"But they might be listening."

"At one a.m.? Unless they're vampires, they should be sound asleep." He nuzzled her neck.

"We might wake them. The children, too."

"We'll be quiet. Or at least I will. You're on your own." Greg was kissing her again, short, soft kisses.

Jane wanted more. With her lips, her body, she communicated her hunger. And Greg answered her plea. Quietly, as promised, but oh, so satisfyingly.

"Mmm." Hours later a sleepy Jane snuggled into a strong, furry chest, reveling in the masculine hands stroking her arms, the muscular male thighs next to hers, the lips brushing her temple. Lost in a world of delight, she twisted her head to meet those lips.

Somewhere in the middle of that meeting—that long, passionate kiss—she awakened fully and opened her eyes. A rosy dawn illuminated the room through the drapes and it was Greg's arms holding her, Greg's body against hers, Greg's lips on hers. "Mmm," she said. "I was afraid it was all a dream."

Jane wasn't up yet and the rest of the household was sleeping late as well when Greg made his way to the kitchen for a solitary cup of coffee. He brewed a pot, then poured a mug for himself as he switched on the radio and tried to focus on the morning news. He couldn't concentrate.

He and Jane were now lovers. Greg asked himself what this meant. Their marriage had started off on such an unusual note, to say nothing of a number of false premises—her concealed identity, his pretended indifference to her. Getting their house in order was way overdue. He needed to let her know how he truly felt about her.

He had her as a wife. He had her as a lover. It was time to banish the fears of losing her and settle for what fate handed him. If he were given only one more day to love her, it would have to be sufficient. If God granted them a thousand days, he'd be truly blessed.

The past was gone and the future was out of his hands. Greg was determined to start living in the present, to appreciate what he had at the moment. As he sat thinking about what he wanted to tell Jane, he heard the footfalls of Jim and Renee on the stairs. Time to put on his company face. It wouldn't be easy forestalling the talk with Jane, but he'd simply have to exercise patience, something he had in short supply. "Good morning, folks," he said. "Sleep well?"

After breakfast Jane's parents departed and Greg asked Elton and Nita to come get the twins and entertain them for a while. "We need to talk," he told Jane.

She'd been expecting as much. All morning Greg had been preoccupied, restive. Luckily her parents didn't know him well enough to pick up on the vibes, but Elton had. It didn't take him more than five minutes in Greg's company to observe that "you're as nervous as a long-tailed cat in a roomful of rocking chairs." Greg blamed an overdose of caffeine, along with the stress of meeting his new in-laws.

The explanation may have fooled Elton, but Jane

knew better. She knew the reason for Greg's anxiety. How could she fail to when it was difficult disguising her own apprehensions about their lovemaking? Last night had changed so much—for her anyway. Greg had to be affected, too.

From her experience and everything she'd read, a man's and a woman's reaction to sex was different. For her, it meant emotional commitment. Not the contractual kind she and Greg already had, but something deeper. She would never have "made love" to Greg if she didn't love him. Although he'd used pretty words last night, that didn't necessarily mean they came from the heart, or that he felt as strongly as she did. The purpose of this talk could be to reiterate his position on that issue.

Determined to get in the first word, Jane started in the minute Elton, Nita and the children were gone. "If you're worried about me reading too much into last night, please rest easy." She sat on the edge of the family room sofa as she spoke. "I know the difference between love and..."

"Is that what you think?" Greg interrupted, sitting down beside her and stretching an arm across the back of the sofa. "That there's no love?"

"I don't know what to think," she admitted.

"Then let me tell you because I've figured it all out." He smiled. "One thing you need to know, Mrs. Merrifield, is that you've just bought yourself a ranch. I'm going to see that your name's added to the deed along with mine."

"That's not necessary."

"Yes, it *is* necessary. I realize you don't *need* anything of mine, but the Circle G is damn well going to be partly yours whether you want it or not.''

''I want it.''

''Thought you did. So that's that on topic one.''

''And topic two? What else do you wish to talk about?''

''Actually talking is losing its appeal real fast,'' Greg said. ''Being this close makes me want to haul you back upstairs to bed.''

The tender look in his eyes imbued her with confidence. Going back to bed was delightful to contemplate. Definitely better than quarreling over money or her career or who did what to whom.

Greg brushed his lips across her forehead. ''But first I have to know, to be certain… Are you really happy here, Janie? Homemaker isn't much of a career statement after the heady world of modeling. Are you sure you want to turn loose of what you had?''

''Absolutely positive,'' she confirmed. ''I know what I want, Greg. After almost twenty years of that 'heady world' as you call it, I knew it was time to quit. And even if I hadn't, Carvel nudged me along in making that call.''

''How'd they do that?''

''By firing me.''

''You were canned?''

Jane nodded. ''So you see, I wasn't simply on a hiatus from work when we met—I had just been cut loose from my long-time sponsor.''

To Jane's amazement, Greg laughed. ''Well, I guessed something was amiss with your employment, but nothing close to this. Boy, have I got a lot to learn."

"Most husbands and wives are a little better acquainted than we were."

"And we're going to start fixing that right now. I want to know everything there is to know, Jane. All those things we should have talked about before."

"You know all the salient points already. We can cover the rest later." She smiled flirtatiously. "Didn't you mention something about going back to bed? For some reason, I didn't get much sleep last night and I could use a nap."

The man leaning against the doorbell that afternoon was a stranger to Greg. Possibly a lost tourist or someone having car trouble, he thought. The Circle G, being off the beaten path, wasn't a target of drop-in visitors or salespeople. "May I help you?" Greg said.

"Hope so. I've been traipsing around half the countryside trying to find this place. "I'm looking for Jane Jarrett. This is where she lives, isn't it?"

Greg nodded. "Yep. But it's no longer Jarrett. She's Mrs. Merrifield now." Greg couldn't help but emphasize the *Mrs.* part. Even though the man standing in front of him was friendly and outgoing, there was a threat about him. Balding, and overweight enough to challenge the seams of his natty white suit, he would be innocuous, except for the fact he wore the self-assured aura of a man used to manipulating people.

"Jane isn't at home," Greg said. He didn't explain that she'd be back any minute as she'd just driven over to the Jones's to pick up the twins.

"If you don't mind, I'll wait. Ron Gold." He stuck out his hand. "Jane's agent."

Reluctantly Greg accepted the handshake, inviting Ron in and offering refreshment. The agent agreed to a cup of coffee.

"Nice place you have here," Ron commented, looking around the den as he sipped his coffee. "Of course, it's a real leap of the imagination to picture J.J., er Jane, on a ranch."

"She seems to like it." Greg felt his hackles rise. The man was polite to a point, but there was condescension in his manner. The urbane guy visiting his country cousins—and looking down his nose the whole time.

"Maybe she thinks she's happy, but what I have here ought to tempt her away for a few weeks." Ron pulled a sheaf of papers from his briefcase. "Carvel wants her back. Boy, do they ever want her back."

"They don't deserve her after the way they treated her," Greg argued.

"I think the money they're offering will serve as penance." Ron quoted a seven-digit figure that made the hair on Greg's neck stand on end. *Damn.* Jane could buy and sell him earning that kind of money. Hell, she could buy half the Panhandle if she felt like it.

No wonder she hadn't blinked an eye over paying off his loan. And here was her agent upping the ante even more. Greg longed to kick Ron Gold's ample rump off the Circle G and warn him that it would be pistols at fifty paces if he ever set foot on the property again. Fat lot of good it would do him, though. If Jane was in such demand as a model, she'd learn about the offer soon enough and despise him for trying to hide it from her. He couldn't keep her his prisoner. But to lose her now...

The slam of a car door caught Greg's attention. He'd been so busy contemplating the possibilities ahead that he hadn't even heard her drive up. "Jane's home," he told Ron and the two headed outside to greet her. Only forced civility kept the men from elbowing each other as they eagerly rushed to her.

"Well, hello, Ron," Jane said with surprise as she started taking the twins out of the car. She handed Sean over to Greg with a tense smile. "And to what do we owe the honor?" she asked, turning to Ron.

"I've come to fetch you," Ron said breathlessly. "This was the sort of news I had to deliver in person, J.J. dearest. Carvel realizes they made a humongous mistake. They want you back. Your public is clamoring for you. I've got the contracts with me. Just sign on the dotted line and you'll be reporting to Paris within ten days."

"Impossible," Jane said, shaking her head. "In case you haven't noticed, Ron, I'm a mother now. Sean and Sarah need me *here,* not half a world away."

"So? Other mothers work. Get a baby-sitter. Hire a nanny. Let *him*—" Ron pointed an accusatory finger at Greg "—take care of them the same way he did before he lured you into his lair."

"Don't be so dramatic." Jane was used to dealing with Ron, but he did tend to go over the top at times, and for people outside of the business, he took a bit of getting used to. From the look on Greg's near-florid face, he wasn't getting used to Ron at all—it was obvious he'd like to punch out the agent's lights.

They went inside and Jane asked Ron to wait while she put the twins down for a nap. When she returned to the den, she expected Greg to be there also, but he wasn't. "Your husband *excused* himself," Ron twittered, as though he'd scored some sort of coup by getting rid of Greg.

"He *is* my husband, Ron. I love Greg Merrifield too much to be away from him a second longer than I have to. So you might as well pack up those contracts and forget your percentage, because I don't intend to sign anything. I'm through with modeling. My life is here."

"Pish. This is just a phase you're going through. You'll be ready to come back within the year."

"I don't think so."

Ron gave an extravagant sigh. "Oh my dear J.J., your devotion to...to *this* is enchanting. Nevertheless, I'm going to forget everything you've said and give you some time to think over what you'd be walking away from. I'll call you tomorrow for an answer."

"It won't be any different."

"I'll call anyway." With that, Ron gathered up his papers, stuffed them into the briefcase and left.

Greg stood at the kitchen window, hands propped against the frame as he watched the man drive away. He felt as if the wind had been knocked out of him.

Backing away from the window, he picked up the mug of coffee he poured earlier. Cold. Dumping the contents into the sink, Greg went in search of Jane. He found her upstairs in the nursery, picking up first Sean, then Sarah and hugging them to her, before laying them back in the cribs and patting their backs. It was unlike Jane to risk awakening the twins when they were sleeping. *Is that a good-bye?*

Greg made his way back downstairs and stood there, leaning against the newel post, as he waited for her to join him.

Jane needed to touch her children for reassurance. It frightened her to realize how close she'd come to missing out on all this. If Carvel had made their offer sooner, her life would have continued ticking along on the same old path—a path of emptiness as far as she was concerned. Now that she'd held her children, Jane wanted to hold her husband, to have him hold her.

Halfway down the stairs, she spotted Greg. His forbidding expression caught her off guard. The past twenty-four hours had convinced Jane she and Greg had come to understand each other, that a happy future together was finally assured. Apparently Greg viewed Ron's visit as voiding that understanding. She'd just have to show him he was wrong.

"Well, is Paris on your itinerary?"

"I thought *this* is where I'm supposed to be from now on."

"That's before your agent burst on the scene with a contract in his hand and dollar talk in every other word. His visit may have changed things."

"It changed nothing. You heard me tell Ron I wasn't interested. You thought he'd persuade me otherwise?"

"It's a lot of money."

"So? I've been earning a lot of money most of my life. Did you really think a little thing like a few more dollars could induce me to leave the ranch?"

"That and a chance to revive your image. Get your place on top of the heap back."

"Think again. None of that brought me happiness before and it wouldn't now. Everything I need is here."

"Are you sure? Money turns most people's heads. Even the heads of people like you who are already loaded with it."

"I can't understand why it's so hard for you to believe me. I've had my fifteen minutes of fame. You, Sean and Sarah make me happy. I love you, Greg. Why do you want to force me to leave?"

"Force you?" Greg gave a bitter chuckle. "I've been torn up inside thinking you were probably ready to start packing—that you couldn't pass up this chance to go back and rub Carvel's mistake in its corporate face. But how do I compete with all that dough?"

"There's no competition. You've scored a perfect ten—Carvel a big fat zero." She smiled and draped her arms around his neck. "Now why don't you claim your prize?"

Doing just that, he sank down on the stair steps, taking her with him. "I couldn't bear losing you, Janie. I love you more than I thought possible." His kisses supported the words.

Reluctantly interrupting the embrace, Greg rose from the steps. "Don't move...I'll just be a second. I have a present for you." He rushed toward his office, quickly returning with a small gift-wrapped package. "I bought this before our wedding, but there hasn't been a good time to give it to you. I came up with this fancy honeymoon setting for doing it, then all hell broke loose and..."

She opened the package and pulled out a gold band with four oval stones—two diamonds, an emerald and a sapphire—set side by side.

"Sometimes people have mother's rings set with the birthstones of their children. This is a *family* ring with all of our birthstones. Sean and Sarah were born in April so the diamonds are for them. The emerald represents you and the sapphire me."

She placed the ring on her finger and moved it to catch the light "I...I'm overwhelmed. It's wonderful, beautiful."

He grinned. "Do you really like it?"

"I love it."

Greg pulled her toward him and Jane kissed him fervently, weeks of pent-up love allowed full expression.

"Does it show how deeply I love you? I realize now that's what I was trying to say when I chose it. I love you, Janie."

"Oh, Greg. I love you, too. I wish I had some

way to show you how much, a way as perfect as this ring." She kissed him again, long and lovingly.

When their lips parted, he said, "That's a darn good start. Besides, you've shown your love every day, in so many small ways. And two hundred and fifty thousand big ones." Smiling, Greg kissed her once more. "Mrs. Merrifield, will you stay with me forever, will you be my wife and the mother of my children?"

It sounded very much like a marriage proposal, a marriage proposal from a man in love. Jane's answer required no deliberation. "Forever," she echoed.

Hours later Greg lay in the dark of night studying Jane as she slept beside him. His heart was overflowing. Watching her, he realized that true love was possible more than once—if you happened to be a very lucky man. *And Merrifield, you're one lucky son of a gun.* He leaned over and kissed his sleeping wife, then lay back smiling.

Head Down Under for twelve tales of heated romance in beautiful and untamed Australia!

Here's a sneak preview of the first novel in THE AUSTRALIANS

Outback Heat by Emma Darcy
available July 1998

'HAVE I DONE something wrong?' Angie persisted, wishing Taylor would emit a sense of camaraderie instead of holding an impenetrable reserve.

'Not at all,' he assured her. 'I would say a lot of things right. You seem to be fitting into our little Outback community very well. I've heard only good things about you.'

'They're nice people,' she said sincerely. Only the Maguire family kept her shut out of their hearts.

'Yes,' he agreed. 'Though I appreciate it's taken considerable effort from you. It is a world away from what you're used to.'

The control Angie had been exerting over her feelings snapped. He wasn't as blatant as his aunt in his prejudice against her but she'd felt it coming through every word he'd spoken and she didn't deserve any of it.

'Don't judge me by your wife!'

His jaw jerked. A flicker of some dark emotion destroyed the steady power of his probing gaze.

'No two people are the same. If you don't know that, you're a man of very limited vision. So I come from the city as your wife did! That doesn't stop me from being an individual in my own right.'

She straightened up, proudly defiant, furiously angry with the situation. 'I'm *me*. Angie Cordell. And it's time you took the blinkers off your eyes, Taylor Maguire.'

Then she whirled away from him, too agitated by the explosive expulsion of her emotion to keep facing him.

The storm outside hadn't yet eased. There was nowhere to go. She stopped at the window, staring blindly at the torrential rain. The thundering on the roof was almost deafening but it wasn't as loud as the silence behind her.

'You want me to go, don't you? You've given me a month's respite and now you want me to leave and channel my energies somewhere else.'

'I didn't say that, Angie.'

'You were working your way around it.' Bitterness at his tactics spewed the suspicion. 'Do you have your first choice of governess waiting in the wings?'

'No. I said I'd give you a chance.'

'Have you?' She swung around to face him. 'Have you really, Taylor?'

He hadn't moved. He didn't move now except to make a gesture of appeasement. 'Angie, I was merely trying to ascertain how you felt.'

'Then let me tell you your cynicism was shining through every word.'

He frowned, shook his head. 'I didn't mean to hurt you.' The blue eyes fastened on hers with devastating sincerity. 'I truly did not come in here to take you down or suggest you leave.'

Her heart jiggled painfully. He might be speaking the truth but the judgements were still there, the judgements that ruled his attitude towards her, that kept her shut out of his life, denied any real sharing with him, denied his confidence and trust. She didn't know why it meant so much to her but it did. It did. And the need to fight for justice from him was as much a raging torrent inside her as the rain outside.

Looking For More Romance?

Visit Romance.net

Look us up on-line at: http://www.romance.net

Check in daily for these and other exciting features:

View all
current titles,
and purchase
them on-line.

Hot off
the press

What do the
stars have in
store for you?

Horoscope

Hot
deals

Exclusive offers
available only at
Romance.net

Plus, don't miss our interactive quizzes,
contests and bonus gifts.

PWEB

Take 4 bestselling love stories FREE

Plus get a FREE surprise gift!

Special Limited-time Offer

Mail to Harlequin Reader Service®

3010 Walden Avenue
P.O. Box 1867
Buffalo, N.Y. 14240-1867

YES! Please send me 4 free Harlequin Romance® novels and my free surprise gift. Then send me 6 brand-new novels every month, which I will receive months before they appear in bookstores. Bill me at the low price of $2.90 each plus 25¢ delivery and applicable sales tax if any*. That's the complete price and a savings of over 10% off the cover prices—quite a bargain! I understand that accepting the books and gift places me under no obligation ever to buy any books. I can always return a shipment and cancel at any time. Even if I never buy another book from Harlequin, the 4 free books and the surprise gift are mine to keep forever.

116 HEN CE63

Name	(PLEASE PRINT)
Address	Apt. No.
City	State	Zip

This offer is limited to one order per household and not valid to present Harlequin Romance® subscribers. *Terms and prices are subject to change without notice. Sales tax applicable in N.Y.

UROM-696   ©1990 Harlequin Enterprises Limited

From the high seas to the
Scottish Highlands,
when a man of action
meets a woman of spirit
a battle of wills—
and love—ensues!

Ransomed Brides

This June, bestselling authors Patricia Potter and
Ruth Langan will captivate your imagination with this
swashbuckling collection. Find out how two men of action
are ultimately tamed by two feisty women who prove
to be *more* than their match in love and war!

SAMARA by Patricia Potter

HIGHLAND BARBARIAN
by Ruth Langan

Available wherever Harlequin and Silhouette
books are sold.

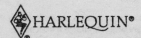 HARLEQUIN®  *Silhouette*®

Look us up on-line at: http://www.romance.net

HREQ0698

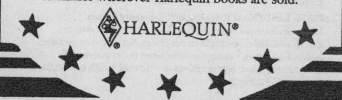

Presents
Extravaganza
25 YEARS!

It's our birthday and we're celebrating....

Twenty-five years of romance fiction
featuring men of the world and captivating women—
Seduction and passion guaranteed!

Not only are we promising you three months of terrific
books, authors and romance, but as an added **bonus**
with the retail purchase of two Presents® titles,
you can receive a special one-of-a-kind keepsake.
It's our gift to you!

Look in the back pages of any Harlequin Presents® title,
from May to July 1998, for more details.

Available wherever Harlequin books are sold.

HARLEQUIN®

Look us up on-line at: http://www.romance.net   HP25BPA

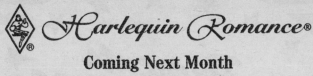

ℋarlequin Romance®

Coming Next Month

#3511 BIRTHDAY BRIDE Jessica Hart
Sexy, glamorous... Claudia tried to think of three good things about
turning thirty. Having to pretend to be David Stirling's bride wasn't
one of them. But for the next few weeks she was stuck with him and
the pretense. And perhaps, at her age, sexy, glamorous and *wed* was an
improvement?

We're delighted to bring you a special new series in Harlequin Romance
and Presents all about...

The Big Event! *One special occasion—that changes your life forever.*

#3512 A KISS FOR JULIE Betty Neels
Julie enjoyed her work as a medical secretary, so it was a nasty surprise
when her elderly boss announced he was retiring. She was partly
reassured when told that Professor Simon van der Driesma was willing to
keep her on—but Simon turned out to be a very different proposition....

#3513 THE BACHELOR AND THE BABIES Heather MacAllister
When Harrison Rothwell is left holding his brother's baby—well, two
babies to be exact—he decides to demonstrate that his rules of business
management can be applied to any situation. Trouble is, his tiny
nephews won't take orders from any boss! Which is where Carrie Brent
comes in. She may be totally disorganized but when it comes to rug
rats—she's a natural! Can she convince Harrison that rules are made to
be broken?

Get ready to meet the world's most eligible bachelors: they're sexy,
successful and, best of all, they're all yours!

Bachelor Territory: *There are two sides to every story...and now it's
his turn!*

#3514 LAST CHANCE MARRIAGE Rosemary Gibson
After one disastrous marriage, Clemency Adams had vowed to
give up men and concentrate on her career. Her next-door neighbor,
Joshua Harrington, was equally determined not to marry again.
Unfortunately, these new neighbors were finding it difficult to fight
their growing attraction for one another....